CANDLELIGHT REGENCY SPECIAL

CANDLELIGHT REGENCIES

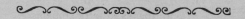

THE
DUKE'S
WARD

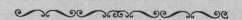

Samantha Lester

A CANDLELIGHT REGENCY SPECIAL

With thanks to Jerry Hopkins
and Pauline Coonrod Hart—
two of the loveliest librarians ever created.

And to Linda Stalker Hanson,
who died before her time.

Published by
Dell Publishing Co., Inc.
1 Dag Hammarskjold Plaza
New York, New York 10017

ISBN 0-440-11925-1

Printed in the United States of America

First printing—October 1980

THE
DUKE'S
WARD

CHAPTER ONE

Anastasia Griffith sat quietly watching the old man on the bed. Her eyes closed, then fluttered open. She yawned, bringing a hand up to cover her mouth. From another portion of the house the sound of a door opening and closing came to her. Sweeping the long strands of auburn hair from her face, she straightened.

"Cora?" she called softly, so as not to waken the sleeping man.

"And who else would it be?" asked the short, heavyset woman as she entered the sleeping chamber. "Ah, Stacey, you've spent another night without sleep. Come, to your bed. There is nothing you can do more than what you have. Your father is of the age where . . ." She broke off at a moan from the man on the bed. Instantly both women's attention went to the frail figure.

"Stacey, lass," the old man got out, his eyes fluttering open. "Stacey, I feel it is the end. You must listen and heed what I say." He breathed heavily for several moments.

"Oh yes, Father," the girl answered, moving closer to her father's lips. "What is it?"

The old man coughed once, and she wiped the spittle from the corner of his mouth. "It was far better that I leave you, lass," he said. "But listen you. Upon my passing, there are to be no tears. You must send notice to the Duke of Essler, immediately. Hear me, lass, for I would not leave this world knowing you were to be uncared for."

"I hear, Father," she answered, passing a hand over his forehead to smooth the thinning hair. "But who is this Duke of Essler, Father?"

"He is . . . " the old man began. Then a gurgling sound came from his throat, followed by a rush of air. He lay still.

"Oh, Cora," the girl moaned, a hand going to her bosom. "Is it the end?"

The older woman moved forward to clutch the wrist of the old man. Straightening, she nodded, placing an arm around the shoulders of the girl. "It is, lass. Your father has gone to join your mother whom he loved so much. It is a blessing, for he has known much pain this five days past. Come, lass, leave his side. It was his wish that you remain brave." So saying, she reached a hand to close the unseeing eyes of the dead man.

"I shall miss him terribly," the girl said, stifling a sob. "Oh, that he should go when so many of so little value live on. It is beyond understanding." Tears flowed down her cheeks as she spoke.

"Come, lass," Cora said softly, helping her ward from the chair. "It was his request that tears not be shed."

The girl nodded. "The tears are for myself and my loss, Cora. My father needs no one to cry for him. He fulfilled the part he was meant to play on this earth, and he did it splendidly."

"That he did," the woman agreed. "Now, come. There are things which must be seen to ere this day is over. Take you to your bed and rest. If the tears are to come, they will last only until sleep overtakes you. I shall see to the arrangements once you are abed."

The girl allowed herself to be led to her quarters and thus to bed, saying, "There will be no sleep for me, Cora, my heart aches for my father."

"Cease your talking, girl. Close your eyes and allow nature to release you from the strain of the last days," was the answer as the older woman drew a coverlet over the girl's lower limbs.

"Ah, that he might have lived to . . ." The girl's voice faded to nothing as the demands of total exhaustion claimed her.

"Sleep, Stacey lass," Cora said, a smile of sorrow on her face as she watched the slow, steady breathing of the girl.

Minutes later, certain that the girl would sleep for some time, Cora left the house and made her way afoot to the village of Brensloe just a mile away. There she saw to the needs of burial and sent a messenger away toward London. Then she joined the men on the funeral wagon to return to the farm of which she had been a part for twenty years.

Upon returning, she went to the girl's room where she assured herself that Stacey had not awakened during the three hours of her absence. Then, with a finger to her lips calling for silence, she directed the men to the death room and watched as they removed the body of the old man. When they'd taken their leave, the abigail removed all the bedclothes from the deathbed and replaced them with fresh linen. Then she retired to the kitchen and placed water over the fire for tea.

It was fully an hour later when Stacey came from the bedroom, rubbing her eyes and asking, "Have I slept the day away, Cora?"

"You've barely slept enough to warrant you rest at all, lass," the abigail answered, rising to pour a cup of tea for the girl. "Your father's remains have been moved to the village to be made ready for burial. I did at the same time send a message to the Duke of Essler as your father wished. Is there anything I can do to ease your plight, Stacey?"

The girl shook her head. "No, Cora. There is little anyone can do to ease the sense of loss at such a thing." She sipped the tea a moment, then met the abigail's eyes. "What of this Duke of Essler, Cora? Why was it of such importance to Father that I contact him?"

The older woman shrugged. "I call to memory that when you were but a tot, this duke came upon the property. Your father at that time said he was third cousin, I believe."

"But what of this pressing need for me to contact him? I am in my twentieth year. Did Father believe me in need of assistance to operate this farm?"

"I know not the answer to your questions, lass. Now, drink your tea. There is much to be done regarding the proper disposal of your father's affairs. We shall have to scan every bit of paper in his desk and file box to ascertain what creditors, if any, need be notified. We shall also pay particular attention to any letters of indebtedness owed your father. Those we shall at once demand payment from. For by your words, I take it you mean to remain here and uphold the property as you have helped your father do for the seven years past."

The girl nodded. "Of course, Cora. What else would you have me do? The land is mine as it was Father's. I shall take the pride in it he always did."

An expression of sadness came over the abigail's features. "Ah, lass, have you no desire to visit the city? Is there nothing in you that suggests the need for a helpmate?"

"Helpmate?" the girl echoed. "Do you refer to the dandies who spend their time ahorse chasing foxes, Cora? Would you have me travel to the city to capture such a useless one? From what I have learned these seven years past, I would prefer to support myself and you rather than have such a one about."

The older woman chuckled softly at the tirade. "Ah, lass, all men are not as those you describe.

There are those who are worthy of any woman's devotion."

"And now you refer to your own Rufus," the girl answered. "But I fear, he was one of a sort. Had he lived, perhaps he might have trained others in the manner you speak of as his own."

The abigail sat silently for a long moment, her eyes misting in memory. Then she nodded. "True, Rufus was a gentle man and a helpmate beyond compare. I agree there are none of the young bucks today who could match him for manliness. Would that you could have known him, lass."

"And that the both of us could have known my mother," the girl added. "For Father did always say she was the finest of persons."

"Come, lass, the searching of memories gains us nothing. Your mother has been dead since the day of your birth and my Rufus before that. There is nothing either of them can do at this time. Come, let us begin the necessary study of your father's papers and records." She cleared the table, leaving only the girl's tea.

Then she moved to another room, returning shortly with a hinged wooden box. "Herein we shall find the extent of your estate or the lack of it. Let us study each page carefully." So saying, she opened the box and removed the papers it held. "Choose one, lass, and read it. If it is of anything to do with a debt owed or due, make mention of it."

The girl nodded. "You are correct, Cora. There is much to be done and perhaps little time to see to it." She lifted a folded sheet and began reading.

An hour later, when the pile of papers had diminished to only a remaining few, Cora suddenly inhaled sharply. "Ah, lass, the answer to your question concerning the Duke of Essler is here."

The girl's head came up. "What is it, Cora?" she demanded. "Pray tell what it is that has taken the color from you."

Without answer the abigail turned the paper and handed it to the girl for her perusal. The room was silent for several minutes, then, groaning slightly, the girl exclaimed, "Ah, it cannot be. Can this document mean what it seems to state?"

Cora nodded. "It would seem so, lass. More's the pity. I never suspected such a thing."

"But is it possible that this land, this house, everything belongs to this duke? Ah, say it is not so, Cora."

The older woman reached across the table to cover the girl's hand. "It is a sorrow, lass, but it appears that the duke has, in fact, owned all for the years your father has worked the ground. This property we occupy is, indeed, a portion of the Essler Dukedom."

The girl sat as if stunned for a long moment before finally meeting the eyes of her abigail. "Then we are without a home to call our own. The duke will surely reclaim his property and see to it that those he deems more capable are in charge of it. What shall we do?"

"There is nothing to do, lass, except wait until

he decides his direction with the property. If, as you suggest, he sees fit to remove us from this place, I shall search for another position in hopes I am as fortunate as with your father and yourself. Perhaps, with God on our side, I will acquire a position for the both of us."

"And what do you remember of this duke, Cora?" Stacey asked. "Might he consider us worthy of remaining and working the land as Father and I have done?"

The older woman considered the suggestion a moment before answering. "There is little chance of such a thing being considered. For there are none who suppose women capable of working as you have been doing these years. No, the duke was of an age beyond your father's when he was here last. There is little chance he would consider allowing one of your years to remain without a husband to assist you."

An oath escaped the girl's lips. "This old man, then, shall come and remove all we have struggled to create," she said in an angry voice. "It is not right that such a thing should be allowed."

"Hush, child," the abigail exclaimed. "Language such as you have used is reserved only for the harlots of the streets and the rum castles. Let not your anger remove all signs of breeding from you."

"Breeding? Of what worth is breeding in light of what we have learned this day, Cora. There would be little difference if I were Queen of England. This ancient duke would remain in control of what I hold dear."

A thoughtful expression captured the older woman's face. "Wait, lass. Recall your father's last words. He did say that he did not wish to depart this world knowing you were to be uncared for. There is a possibility that an agreement was made with this duke to see to your welfare. Come, let us look through the final pages of documents." She lifted one of the two remaining pages and studied it.

"What of it, Cora?" the girl asked as the abigail refolded the sheet and placed it aside.

"It is nothing but a receipt for monies paid by your father for a cow which has long since died." She opened the final sheet and began reading. Minutes later she sighed heavily and met the girl's anxious glance. "It is here, lass. It is an agreement between the duke and your father that his grace see to your well-being until you are wed, should your father reach his end before you take husband."

Color flooded over the girl. "See to my well-being? What is that to mean? What of you? Might this duke not consider making a scullery maid of me as a portion of seeing to my well-being? Have I no say in what manner this is to happen? Must I forgo all to the wishes of this ancient duke who is to take all I believed my own?"

The abigail shrugged. "I know not, lass. There is within this record the wishes of your father, it would seem. He did, those years back, commit this duke and yourself. There is nothing to do but await the duke's word. When he has made his wishes known, we shall better know what is to be done."

The girl's color heightened. "This duke knows little of our way of life. He spends all his time in London. You yourself recall but one visit by him to this place. It is impossible that he will know of anything except the evils of the city."

A chuckle escaped the older woman's lips. She reached to pat the hand of the angry girl. "Now, lass, there is more than evil present in the city. It is a misfortune that you have never visited London to acquaint yourself with the pleasures to be found there. For there are those things and those people the likes of which Brensloe has no match."

The girl fixed her with a questioning glance. "How is it then that Father disliked any and all connected with London?"

The older woman shrugged. "Your father had his reasons, lass. I know not what they were. Suffice to say, he thought only of your welfare in keeping the rumblings of London from you."

It seemed the girl would break into tears. She inhaled sharply. "And now it is my lot to be taken from that which my father deemed best for me to this London to become scullery maid to this ancient duke. Ah, why could my life not have ended with Father's. It would have been the better for all."

"Hush such talk, lass," the abigail scolded. "Judge not the events of the coming days before you become aware of their content. Come, now. Though the future holds little we know of, the toil of this place remains as always. Come, we must see to the animals."

Sadly the girl followed her abigail from the room. "We work not for our own benefit from this moment," she said as they stepped to the open yard. "We toil for one who knows nothing of such things."

CHAPTER TWO

The Dowager Duchess of Essler placed her teacup in its saucer and eyed the tall, dark-haired young man who paced the floor at the fireplace. She smiled with pride as the thought occurred to her that this son of hers was truly a picture of his late father. The eye patch which glistened darkly over his left eye detracted not at all from his handsome appearance, she assured herself. In fact it added to the regal, commanding effect of his broad-shouldered six feet. A son to be proud of, she told herself as he swung to face her.

"So, Mother, what of this message? What is there about it that demands my presence in some distant village?"

"The village is known as Brensloe," she answered, amused at his obvious agitation. "And the demands are those of your father's wishes. It was his desire that his third cousin, Richard Griffith, work the land as his own until the time of his death. Your father and Richard were quite close in their younger days, so close in fact that they were as brothers."

"And so, the man has died," the young man said. "I take it the land now reverts back to Essler. Why must I take myself from these grounds at this moment to lay claim to that which has already been seen to?"

"There was more to the agreement between the late duke and Richard Griffith," the duchess said. "If you will but settle yourself for a period long enough to allow me to acquaint you with the terms of the agreement, I believe you will have a fuller understanding of all." She paused and added, "The wars are at an end, Nigel. Bonaparte is on his island and can no longer cause the world strife. It is time you assumed the duties of your late father as Duke of Essler. Come, sit. Your constant pacing affects me."

Reluctantly he dropped into a chair, saying, "There are those moments when I wonder that the short general allowed himself to be so placed in exile. Also there are times when I consider the responsibilities of the dukedom and would rather be again in the battlefields, where only the freedom of all Europe was at stake." He sighed heavily. "Very well, Mother, acquaint me with whatever is required within the agreement."

She, too, sighed heavily. "To begin, there is the necessity of your visiting each and all of the Essler holdings. Those who work the holdings have been long without evidence of the duke's guidance. But this Griffith affair must be seen to at once." She consulted the message, which had only an hour before been delivered. "It would seem impossible for you to arrive in time for the burial of Richard Griffith, the distance being what it is. You should, however, make your way as soon as possible to Brensloe and attend to the remaining portion of the agreement met by your father and Richard."

"And that entails?" he asked.

She lifted another document and studied it. "It appears there was a child to whom your father promised protection should Richard meet his death. It is a girl child, and your father promised to see to her fortunes until the time she should marry."

The young duke's eyes widened. "A girl child? Am I, then, to be nursemaid to a child until she comes of age to beguile some unsuspecting male into marriage?"

The duchess snorted softly. "The girl child would at this moment be in her twentieth year. She is but seven years your junior. She is, in all likelihood, already wed to one of the country lads of Brensloe. The terms of the agreement, however, require that you see to your responsibility. You must travel to Brensloe and determine what is to be done."

"Would it not be simpler to merely send a message instructing this country husband of my father's ward to continue working the ground in the usual arrangement as with our other holdings, Mother?"

She shook her head. "It will not do, Nigel. You are, and always have been, a caring person. Your concern for others is equal to that of your father. Only the recent wars have brought you to the point of disillusionment with others."

He nodded agreement. "It seems you know me well, Mother. It is true. The childlike trust with which men have placed the short emperor in their island stronghold strikes me as idiotic. They believe their ills to be ended simply because they have placed water between the disease and their shores. I miss my guess if Bonaparte remains long where they have placed him. Ambition such as his cannot be shackled."

"And so you have spent many months telling all members of Parliament who would listen. It is, however, out of your hands. The duties of the Duke of Essler remain, in spite of the accuracy of your predictions. You must see to those who are dependent on you and your judgment. You must take yourself to Brensloe and see to the drawing up of an agreement such as is now held with the people who occupy Essler lands. Such was the friendship of your father and Richard Griffith, that the duke would hear nothing of Richard's paying for use of the land. It has, in effect, been Richard's property all these years."

The young man eyed his mother. "An uncommon agreement between gentlemen," he said. "And a costly one, it would seem, for the House of Essler."

"Your father did not deem it so," was her answer, "for on two occasions, at least, the duke owed his life to Richard Griffith. Thus the agreement to see to his daughter."

Her son raised a hand to adjust the black eye patch. "Ah, Mother, you were always one to omit the very bones of a matter until such time as all were in quandary. Why was no mention made of this strong debt owed by my father to this Griffith fellow? There can, of course, be no question of the agreement. Whatever my father thought due can be little enough payment for the service performed by this Richard Griffith." He got to his feet. "I shall prepare to leave for Brensloe immediately. What would you have me do with this female child should she remain single?"

The duchess fixed him with a serious glance. "She is the daughter of your father's third cousin and friend. If, indeed, she has not married, then she is deserving of her season as are all of the Essler blood. You will return with her and upon viewing her, we shall determine what is to be done. Though in her twentieth year, she shall have her chance to choose well for a husband if there is aught we can do to see to it."

The young duke raised his eye heavenward. "May she be wed and with child," he muttered in mock severity, his lips pulling into a smile as he spoke.

"Enough of your wit," his mother exclaimed, suppressing a smile of her own. "It is none of your affair if I find pleasure in matchmaking."

"I was recalling the results of your last attempt," he said, smiling broadly. "It strikes me such planning and deviousness might well have

23

been the reason for Father taking his leave of this world."

She snorted heavily. "Your father remained outside such intrigues," she said, "as I suspect you will. Men are a bother, to say the least. Why anyone of good sense would wish one for a mate escapes me. Now, enough of your harassment. Go see to the duties of Essler."

"Yes, Mother," he answered, bowing from the waist. "I shall bring this lass to Essler if she yet be without mate. You shall have your pleasure of turning London end for end to allow her a season." He laughed shortly. "I assume she will be heavy beyond belief, with the skin of a reptile to be covered over with cosmetics. Ah, the sorrow I feel for the suitors of London. They know not what awaits them."

She chuckled in spite of herself. "Begone," she said. "You would have all who wish the best for such lasses seem as ogres. Happiness in life depends not on a lass's skin texture, but on what she does to please her mate."

"Yes, Mother," he laughed, turning to leave the room. "I shall return with this scaly creature if she is yet unmarried. Prepare your magic potions that you may turn the world of free men into slavery." He was still laughing as he left.

Behind him the duchess shook her head in dismay at the actions of her only son. Finally, her mood becoming serious, she said aloud, "Ah, Nigel, the potions of which you speak must, in the few years hence, see to your marriage." She thought of the number of young women who had thrown themselves at her son, to no avail, since his return from the wars and shook her head in wonder. "He can see only Bonaparte and the threat therein," she murmured, rising to call to the maid.

The second day following her father's funeral, Anastasia awoke and attired herself for the day. The simple gray dress of the farm woman fit her in such manner to emphasize the curves of her body and her youthful bustline. She took no notice of her appearance. Running a comb carelessly through her tresses, she left her room and called to the abigail.

"In the kitchen, lass," came the answer.

Entering the kitchen, Stacey met the concerned glance of the older woman and said, "You need not concern yourself, Cora. The sadness which ruled me following Father's burial has become a numbness I must live with."

Cora's relief at the words was obvious. Hurriedly she placed breakfast before the girl and then took her own seat at the table. "The flowers at the front should be seen to this day," she said.

The girl nodded. "I shall do it, Cora. I would not have this ancient duke think us lacking in the care of his property."

"Come, lass," the older woman said, "remove the bitterness from your system. It was not the duke's doing. It was your father's concern for you which brought about the contract. It would appear this duke was indeed liberal with your father, for whatever reasons. There was no mention

25

in anything we read of any rents being paid to the man in all these years. Judge him not until you have known him and his intentions."

"He would take my land from me," the girl said stubbornly.

"He would take possession of that which has, all along, been his," Cora corrected. "Now finish your meal and see to the flowers."

CHAPTER THREE

Nigel, Duke of Essler, sent a glance around as the carriage rolled through the countryside. Suddenly he called for the driver to draw the carriage to a stop.

"Yes, your grace?" the driver asked when the duke stepped from the coach.

"I would ride at the lines with you," Nigel said, reaching to pull himself upward to the seat. "The view from within leaves much unseen."

"Yes, your grace," the coachman answered.

Nigel fixed the man with a stern glance. "Tell me, Claude, how long have you served me and my father before me?"

An expression of pride crossed the older man's face. "Thirty-two years I make it, your grace. It was me set you on your first pony, though I doubt you remember it."

"I remember it well, Claude. I remember also

your assistance in the many incidents of my youth which would not bear mentioning. You have always been one worthy of a child's or a man's trust in anything requiring discretion."

"Thank you, your grace," Claude answered, obviously puzzled by the conversation.

"In view of all that has gone before, Claude, it does seem too much for you to continually refer to me as 'your grace.' I tire of the words from the mouth of one so close as yourself. From this moment I would have you use my given name except in the presence of those who wear their noses upward in this world. Are we agreed?"

The proposal took the driver by surprise. He sat in stunned silence for a long moment before saying, "It would not be seemly, your grace. I am but . . ."

"You are but a trusted friend," Nigel snapped. "There were those in the war who had no title but who considered themselves my friends. Friends do not rely on titles. Are we indeed friends, Claude?"

"Oh, yes, your grace. Why, I recall cleaning you of horse dung when you were but a tot ere your mother could lay eyes on you. You were a rapscallion, your grace. Begging your pardon, sir."

Nigel threw back his head and laughed heartily. "There, man. That is what I have reference to. Should one who has cleaned another of dung be constantly expected to refer to him as 'your grace'? It is insane. I will not have it. My name is Nigel. Use it, man."

Reluctantly the driver nodded. "Very well, your grace. If that is your wish."

"It is my wish. Say the name, Claude."

Hesitantly the man said, "Nigel. Yes, your grace, Nigel."

With a shake of his head the duke chuckled. "Well, it is, at least, a beginning. Drive on, Claude. Brensloe is not more than an hour ahead of us. We shall arrive by midday."

The sun was nearing its zenith when the carriage rolled across the Brensloe bridge, struck a hole, and tilted sideways. Clutching for the seat rail, Nigel steadied himself and voiced a curse as the driver brought the horses to a halt.

"Blast!" Claude exclaimed, jumping from the seat to study the broken rear wheel of the carriage. His glance went from the wheel to the duke, and a tone of remorse filled his voice when he said, "My eyes become my enemy, your grace. The hole should have been obvious to one who has driven the distance I have."

Removing himself from the carriage seat to join the driver, the duke studied the wheel for a moment, then cast a glance back toward the bridge at the hole which had brought an abrupt end to their travels. "Blame not yourself, Claude," he said. "There's none could have known of the hole from our direction. Only from this side is it visible." He turned to study the village they had entered. "Perhaps, with good fortune, a wheelwright can be found here. Come, let us see." So saying, he stepped off toward the town, the driver following.

Locating the wheelwright required nothing more than the questioning of the first citizen they met. Making their way to the tradesman's shop, they arranged to have the carriage brought in and the wheel repaired.

"And how soon shall we expect the task done, sir?" Nigel asked.

The wheelwright shrugged. "Who can tell, your grace? The wheel itself must be mended. Following that, the iron of the rim must be forged anew and shrunk to the wheel." He raised his eyes in deep thought and finally added, "I fear it will be near evening, sir."

"Have you no help, man?" Claude demanded. "The duke must be on his way."

"There are few enough in Brensloe who have carriages," came the immediate reply. "Much the less those who care to work on them."

"It will do," the duke said. "Remain to assist the man, Claude. If I can but find directions to the Griffith holdings, I shall see to passage. When the carriage is repaired, you may come for me."

"Is it the house of Richard Griffith you refer to, your grace?" the tradesman asked.

Nigel nodded. "You know of the place then?"

"Certainly, sir. It is but a short distance from Brensloe on the main road." He raised a finger to point down the road they'd been traveling. "Had you not broken the wheel, you would be nearing the site by now."

Nigel nodded thoughtfully. Suddenly a decision formed in his mind, and he said, "Claude, I believe I shall walk to the farm. The exertion will serve my muscles well. When the carriage is ready, come for me."

"Very well, your grace," the driver answered. "In all likelihood a carriage can be rented to take you there if your grace wishes."

"No. I rather relish the walk. I have been too long on my backside at Essler." He set off at a ground-eating pace, the clean-scented air of the countryside filling his nostrils and a sensation of well-being taking him.

The pleasant odors of cooking meat filled the air when Stacey left her work with the flowers and drew water from the well to wash the marks of her labor from her hands and arms. Cora was waiting for her when she entered the house and passed through the front-most rooms to the kitchen.

"Ah, lass, from the expression you wear, the pruning has gone ill. Sit. A hearty meal of pork will make the day appear brighter."

Sinking into a chair at the table, Stacey ran a palm over her forehead and said, "There is nothing ill with the pruning, Cora. It is only the thought that I labor for another's profit that pains me." Suddenly she slammed a hand on the table top. "It is unfair that all which has been done here shall fall into the hands of one who needs it not and is of an age where it matters little. It is unfair!"

Sorrowful understanding etching her face, the

abigail moved to place food before the girl. "There is naught to be done about it, lass. Eat your dinner. It is not in you to allow ruin to come to any upon this place, no matter who is to benefit."

The girl nodded. "It is true, Cora. My life is here. I would have it as Father did, a place of beauty, no matter what it shall require of me. It is only the thought of being forced from this place that puts me in so ill a mood."

"Yes. Well . . . " the abigail began, then stopped at a call from the front of the house. "Now, who can that be?" she wondered aloud as she moved to open the door. Moments later Stacey heard her speak words of cautious greeting. A male voice answered. She turned from her plate in time to see a tall, handsome man with dark hair and a black eye patch ushered into the kitchen by the governess.

"A wayfarer," Cora announced as she waved the newcomer to the table. "Afoot he is, and traveling without bread or drink." She gave her attention to the man. "Sit. There's food enough for you. Though where you are bound from the direction of Brensloe is beyond understanding. There's nothing within two day's travel by carriage in the direction you head."

Stacey realized that she had been staring at the newcomer. Chiding herself for her lack of manners, she nodded to the man and asked, "And have you a name, sir?"

"Nigel," he answered, then paused. "I wish to cause no imposition."

32

Stacey shook her head. "There will be none for your dining with us, sir. The food is prepared in enough abundance for the three of us. At the present time I find my appetite less than it should be."

Nigel studied the auburn hair and green eyes of the lovely girl with an appraising eye. His expression was one of extreme satisfaction when he asked, "And might I know the names of my benefactors, m'lady?"

The title brought a laugh from Stacey. "Not m'lady, sir, Only Anastasia Griffith, a farm lass who has none but a dim future ahead of her." She indicated the abigail. "The caring soul who feeds you is Cora, my companion since the death of my mother some years ago."

At the mention of her name Nigel's eyes widened appreciatively. For a moment he was silent. Then with a smile forming in the corners of his mouth, he asked, "And what is there to bring such a troubled mark to the face of one so young and lovely as you, Lady Anastasia? Surely one of your tender age cannot bear all the troubles of the world on her shoulders."

Cora placed meat and vegetables before him at that moment, saying, "Not the troubles of the world, perhaps, sir, but ills enough for any, no matter what their years."

He sent a glance around the kitchen and shook his head. "I cannot sense how troubles could visit themselves on any who live in such simple beauty as surrounds this house. The flowers at the entrance are of a beauty seldom seen in the best boxes of London. The peace of this place speaks of no ill for those who live here."

Stacey nodded. "True, it is all you say. It means little, though, when one looks forward to nothing more than being forced from . . ." She paused, then said, "My apologies, sir. It would seem I am too ready to share my woes with any and all who become available. Please eat your dinner. The meat is good and you are, I'm sure, eager to continue your travels."

Nigel nodded, the ill-concealed smile still tugging at his lips. "I will partake of the fare offered. I will, then, expect to perform whatever tasks need be done in payment for your hospitality." He fell to eating, aware of the eyes of the two women on him.

"There will be no need for your efforts along such lines, sir," Stacey told him as she, too, began eating.

"It is little enough to do for another in a world as torn as this," Cora added. "It is enough to know that a fellow being shall not go hungry this day."

"We shall see," he answered around a mouthful of food. "It is not in me to take and not repay, whatever the cost."

"Consider that whatever you do not consume will go for naught in any case, sir," the girl told him. "For within the matter of several days, all you see here will be as nothing to the two of us."

"Your meaning escapes me, m'lady," he said. "What is there that could put you in such straits?"

34

Cora ceased eating to say, "The lass is in a way. She has only recently seen to the burial of her father. It was upon his death she found that this land she thought to be her own is in fact the property of one who will surely remove her from it."

His eyes went to Stacey. "Is this true, m'lady?"

She nodded sadly and pushed away from the table. "It is true, sir. The old one may at this very moment be in his carriage bound for Brensloe, intending to take me to London to become a scullery maid—or even worse—in service to him."

Suppressing a laugh, the duke said, "And what of this old one to which you refer? Is he known to you to be so vile as you suggest?"

"It is the terms of an agreement between her father and the Duke of Essler," Cora told him as the girl turned away from the table. "Until the lass is wed, she is to be cared for by the duke."

"But if he is to care for her until she is wed, why does she believe herself destined to become a scullery maid? Perhaps he will become infatuated with her and take her to the bosom of his household as a member of the titled family."

"Hah!" Cora snorted. "I myself have viewed this duke many years back. His age was greater than the girl's father. There's naught he would have for the girl but to make a servant of her in his dotage."

"Oh, must we discuss this?" Stacey cried, turning to face them. "There is nothing to be done for the situation. And you, sir, surely cannot find interest in such things."

"Oh, you wrong me, m'lady. You and your companion have seen fit to treat me as an equal when it was uncalled for. If there is anything I can do to assist you, I shall be happy to do so." He paused, his manner thoughtful. "I shall wait for the coming of this Duke of Essler. When properly approached, he will, I am certain, take you to London and present you to the duchess so that you might be attired and presented as a lady of rank, such as your beauty deserves."

Both women looked at him as if he'd gone mad. "You suggest, sir, that you, a wayfarer without the bare necessities of even horse and extra garb, might speak to a duke and convince him of what you say?" Stacey asked. "You surely have come to the end of your senses. There are none of such title who would do more than strike you upon your head should you speak to them."

He chuckled aloud. "You do judge the titled ones harshly, m'lady. Though I will not argue there are those who act in the manner suggested by you, I feel there are also those who are of decent attitude toward others. I believe this duke will heed my suggestions and see to your well-being. I should, were I fortunate enough to be the Duke of Essler."

Stacey straightened her shoulders and turned away from him. "Then it is a pity you are not this ancient duke, sir. Now, I fear I must forgo your further imaginings. They do little to help my present mood and nothing toward the completion of the pruning. Enjoy your meal, sir." With that she left the house.

Shaking her head, Cora removed the girl's unfinished meal from the table. She was muttering to herself when she again took her seat across from the man with the eye patch.

"I would like to suggest that the lass and yourself worry for little cause, Cora," he said. "The duke certainly is not as you picture him."

She met his glance. "The presumptions of our minds may agree not at all with your own, sir. However there is little doubt that the man will remove the girl and myself from this farm and place it in the hands of men who seem better fitted to care for it. The property is his and he will wish the gold of profits from it."

Nigel nodded, barely concealing his laughter. "And is he not so entitled, m'lady? For if the lands are his, then a share of the bounty should be his also, should it not?"

"True," she reluctantly agreed. "It is more the removal of the lass from this place which plagues me. For, though she is unaware of it, I feel there will be no place for such as myself within the duke's plans. It turns as a knife in flesh to think of the child without a protectoress."

"But what of the Duchess of Essler?" he asked, thinking of his mother's pleased surprise when he returned to London.

"That lady, for all she might be caring, must be of an age requiring the hands and back of youth to assist her. It will, I fear, be Stacey's position to become a servant to that one, also."

Nigel bent over his plate to prevent outright laughter at this suggestion. When he again had

37

control of himself, he finished the portion of food and stood, saying, "I shall assist the lovely Stacey in her pruning. It would not do for her to offend her lovely hands before the duke arrives."

Cora eyed him up and down. Finally, with suspicion alive in her eyes, she said, "Make no head-turning statements to the girl, sir. She is of her twentieth year, it is true, but she is unused to smooth honey dripping from the tongues of becoming men such as yourself. Do not upset her, for she is troubled enough."

He bowed formally. "My thanks for the meal and the compliment you have just paid, Cora. I assure you, I attempt only to ease the mind of your ward." With that, he smiled broadly and left the house.

Stacey was on her knees pruning a thick rose-bush when he stepped from the house and looked around for her. Hearing his footsteps, she turned, asking, "And is your belly full, sir?"

He nodded. "It is to bursting, m'lady. I would now be allowed to pay for what I have eaten."

"There is no payment due, sir, as I told you."

He moved closer. "Do you not think London would be pleasant for a lovely such as yourself? Would you not enjoy the theater, the dances, and the teas?"

She stood silent for a long moment, aware of a strange sensation brought on by his closeness. Suddenly an unexpected trembling seized her, and she stepped away from him. "That is not to be my lot, I fear, sir. You have, perhaps, been a portion of such affairs?"

"Ah, many times. And I wager one of your beauty would take London by storm—knock it end for end, as it were. Your season would be less than three days gone before you were deluged by offers, unless I miss my guess."

Her eyes widened. "What is this you speak of? You truly are mad, sir. Season? I expect no season. I wish only to be left as I am." Her head dropped at the words. "But that is not to be, I fear."

He chuckled lightly. "I fear you do allow your imaginings to run away with you, m'lady. You have nothing to fear from this duke. Indeed I feel it as though I were he. When he does make his presence known here, I am certain he will take you and your abigail to his heart."

Anger replaced the sadness in her expression. "You, sir, are having jest with me. It is ill pay for the kindness shown you by Cora and myself. I will listen to no more." She turned away from him and again began working at the roses.

"I meant no jest, m'lady," he began, "for in truth I am . . ."

". . . a bore, sir," she cut him off. "Go now. Continue your travels and allow us to await our fortunes in peace, without your rambling thoughts and wit."

"But, m'lady, I . . ."

"I will listen to nothing more," she snapped, anger bringing color to her face. Turning away from him, she stamped into the house, leaving him alone in the yard.

"Ah," he murmured, "you will find much to

amaze you in that one, Mother. She will, I fear, upturn the House of Essler within a day of her arrival." The thought voiced, he turned and stepped through the gate toward the village of Brensloe.

Meanwhile, upon seeing the anguish upon her ward's features, Cora sped to her side. "What is it, lass? What has happened?" she demanded. "Has the wayfarer been unseemly to your person?"

Stacey shook her head, for the moment too angry to speak. "No, Cora," she said finally. "His manner to me was one of wit and humor, but his foul pleasure in our plight angered me. It was of some surprise to me, for I had thought him a gentleman."

Cora agreed. "He did seem a gentleman, lass." She moved to the window and cast a glance outside. "Hah, he takes his leave of this place. And it seems he has thought the better of his travels for the day. He returns in the direction of Brensloe. He'll find the inn there anything but comforting." She turned back to Stacey and took note of the expression on the girl's face. "What is it, lass?"

"There was a moment when he stood close to me, Cora," she answered. "My very being seemed tipped end up and over. It was a strange feeling such as I have never known."

The older woman's eyes narrowed. "Did he lay hands on your person, child?"

The girl looked at her in confusion. "No, Cora. Why should such a thing occur to you? What would have been his purpose? I spoke of my own odd feelings, not of him."

Cora remained silent for a long moment. Then,

meeting the girl's steady glance, she said, "He was handsome, though lacking one eye. There have been none in your acquaintance to match his appearance. It is infatuation you feel, lass. Concern yourself not. There will be others to turn your head."

"Infatuation?" Stacey repeated the word, her color heightening. "You suggest I felt fondness for a wayfarer who was not known to me but an hour ago? I feel your imaginings to be the match of his, Cora. It was simply the small amount of food taken by me which upset my system." She returned to the roses, an expression of perplexity on her face.

Behind her Cora smiled tightly. "Ah, lass," she murmured. "So little is known to you of your own feelings. Would that the world could open to you and allow your caring ways their due." Sadly she turned back to the washing of the dishes from the noonday meal.

"By all that's holy," Nigel exclaimed as the dust of the road rose in puffs under his every step. "She will be the toast of London. Mother will have little problem matching her with any she chooses." He laughed aloud in memory of the references to the Duke of Essler by the two women. "Well," he said at length, "it is true. I near an age where a woman such as the Stacey lass would be a welcome servant to have around." He chuckled heartily to himself and quickened his pace.

CHAPTER FOUR

It was midafternoon when he arrived at the wheelwright's shop. Claude sat on a long, wooden bench, watching the tradesman's efforts. He stood quickly when Nigel stepped into the building.

"Ah, your grace, you have returned."

Nigel nodded and sent a glance down over his dusty clothes. "It would seem I have, indeed, Claude. It would also seem I have brought most of the road's dust with me. How goes the repair of the wheel?"

The wheelwright looked up from his work to say, "But a bit more time, your grace. The rim is being shrunk into place this moment."

"Excellent," Nigel said, his attention going back to Claude. "I have met the Lady Griffith, Claude. She is, to say the least, like a breath of fresh spring

43

air. I believe my mother will find she has her hands full with that one."

"And, sir," the driver asked, "is she of a happy state of mind for having met your grace?"

A chuckle escaped the duke's lips. "Her distaste for the Duke of Essler is bested only by her dislike for the total of the titled heads of all Europe. She would have the Duke of Essler taken from the face of the earth if it were within her power."

"Eh, what is it you say, sir? Did she show disfavor to your person?"

Laughter boiled to the surface as Nigel recalled his recent experiences with the two women. "Be at your ease, Claude. They took me for a wayfarer—a rather stupid one at that. It is uncanny the thoughts which enter heads concerning the unknown."

"Beg pardon, sir?"

"The two women—this Stacey and her abigail—are certain the Duke of Essler is in his dotage. They know in their own minds that he will come and make slaves of them."

Claude fixed him with a questioning glance. "Your meaning escapes me, your grace. They believe you will enslave them?"

Nigel laughed heartily. "Ah, Claude, I left them without enlightening them as to my identity, though at one time, I attempted, without success, to make myself known. The lass is consumed with fear of what is to become of her and her abigail. Ah, well, once the wheel is repaired, we shall return to them and place their minds at ease."

Obviously confused at his superior's manner,

Claude nodded. "As you will, your grace. Am I to understand the lady is angry with your grace?"

"Rather she is angry with what she supposes the Duke of Essler to be," Nigel answered. "You shall be further enlightened when the wheel is again in place and we are at the Griffith farm. I believe you will be pleasantly surprised at the girl child whom my father promised to protect."

Stacey and Cora stood at the well drawing water for the animals when sounds of the coach reached them. Hesitating in their efforts, they glanced toward the road.

"A fine carriage, from the looks of it," Cora said, shading her eyes with a hand.

"And traveling much too fast," Stacey added. Then she gasped. "Oh, Cora. Is it possible the carriage is that of the Duke of Essler? Is it possible that he has come so soon to remove us from this land?"

Cora frowned. "It is possible, lass—aye, probable in fact. Even now the carriage slows."

The coach drew to a stop at the gate, and the driver stepped to the ground to open the door.

"Come, lass," Cora said, taking the girl's arm. "It would seem we must greet this duke. Take the grimace of hatred from your expression. It will help nothing to anger the man." She led the reluctant girl toward the gate and carriage.

They were within a half-dozen steps of the gate when Nigel stepped from the carriage and sent a glance around the area. His eyes found them, and he raised a hand in greeting. "Ah, Anastasia and

45

Cora," he called. "How delightful to see the both of you again so soon. Would it be possible for a wayfarer to partake of food and drink before continuing on his travels?"

Both women stopped in their tracks for a moment. Their mouths fell open as they stared first at the carriage, then at Nigel. Finally Stacey regained her wits and moved forward saying, "And, Nigel, are you of such wealth that you choose to rent so fine a carriage to complete your travels?" She came face to face with him. "And have you returned here to continue your cutting wit at our expense?"

At that moment Claude, an expression of confusion riding his features asked, "Shall I see to the horses, your grace?"

Chuckling, Nigel nodded. "Yes, Claude. Then, perhaps, the ladies will allow both of us to drink from their well."

Stacey's eyes opened wide. She flung a quick look at Claude, then brought her attention back to Nigel. "Your . . . your grace?" she got out. "What?"

He bowed from the waist. "Your servant, m'lady. I truly am the ancient ogre known as the Duke of Essler. As you predicted, I am here to place you and your abigail in bondage to my person." He raised a hand to stroke his chin in a manner of deep consideration. "Let us study on it. Should manacles and leg irons be used for the two of you or would twenty lashes a day suffice to insure control over you? It is a point to ponder."

Angry color swept into the girl's face. She

opened her mouth, closed it, then in a rush of words said, "You . . . Oh, you. I would . . . Oh!" She inhaled deeply, her anger and embarrassment preventing the utterance of a coherent sentence.

Claude stood in awe of the girl. He looked to the duke, asking, "Your grace, what . . ."

Laughter echoed from Nigel's lips. Again he bowed to Stacey. "My apologies, m'lady. It was unseemly of me to allow you to think as you did on my first visit to your home." He straightened, still laughing, and added, "My man and I truly are in need of refreshment, m'lady."

Cora moved forward at that moment, her face ashen, her manner subdued. She dropped to curtsy before him, saying, "Your grace is welcome."

His laughter gained volume as he looked down at her. "Come, Cora. How is it that you place yourself in such a position before the wayfarer who only hours ago dined at your table as an equal. Rise. Such deference will not do. Your actions do nothing but embarrass me." He bent to take her arm and bring her to a standing position. "Now, the two of you, an apology for my actions is due you. The opinions expressed earlier by you were of such manner that I found it impossible to reveal my identity to you. Suffice it to say, the opinions you expressed of me were, I hope, inaccurate."

At mention of their comments on his earlier visit, color again flooded Stacey's face. "Ah," she got out, "we did not intend . . ."

"Enough," he said. "It is done. I will attempt to live up to the die you have cast for me." He laughed heartily at the expressions on their faces. "Come, ladies. May we drink from your well? There is much to prepare before we take our leave of this place to return to London and present you, Anastasia, to the Duchess of Essler."

Stacey, a hand to her mouth, sighed, "It would seem we have indeed allowed our mouths to bring trouble to us, m'lord. Oh, that it were possible to recall that which was said."

"Or that amends could be made for the harsh words concerning the titled heads," he added.

She studied his face for a moment. "Is it jest you make of us, your grace?" she asked, her manner subdued.

His laughter filled the evening air. "Ah, Anastasia, I must confess my humor has taken firm grip on me where you and Cora are concerned. If only my thirst were quenched, perhaps I could find it possible to control my wit."

At reference to the oft-mentioned drink, both women sighed in embarrassment. "Ah, your grace," Cora said. "Come, allow us to refresh you at our table."

Nigel shook his head sadly, the beginning of a frown on his face. "I tire of your use of the title, ladies. Is it not possible for me to remain as I was but a few hours ago, simply Nigel?"

The women exchanged wondering glances. Finally Stacey said, "It will indeed be difficult, your gr— Nigel. It does take concentration. But, come, you and your man thirst. You might never recover from that thirst if you allow the two of us to continue." She turned to enter the house. Behind her Nigel nodded to Claude and followed her.

When both men had wine before them, Stacey seated herself at the table and studied Nigel for several seconds before asking, "And do you truly mean to take this farm from me, sir?"

Lowering the drink from his lips, he reached to adjust the eye patch and fixed her with a stare from his good eye. He nodded. "I do, indeed, m'lady. A farm such as this is hardly the place for one such as you. You shall travel to London with Claude and myself. There, you will meet and, I am certain, love the Duchess of Essler. She will see to your needs as befits one of the Essler blood."

Stacey was about to speak when a thought overtook her. "And will your wife, the duchess, be as willing that we become portion of her household, sir?"

He laughed shortly at the question. "The duchess is my mother, and she will be delighted. It has been her misfortune to have but one child. She will relish having another underfoot to see to, especially since the first was a boy. She would have the pleasure of fitting a daughter, no matter what age, as she would a doll. Yes, she will be pleased."

Stacey met Cora's glance, then asked, "And did not the duchess wish to travel with you to view this child before she became as mother to her?"

Nigel shrugged. "She found it more to her liking to remain in London and await your coming.

She is, I am afraid, not of a mood to take herself from the city."

"Is she ailing, my lord?" Cora asked.

Again Nigel shook his head. "Only from the concern for a son who cares not enough for his position and duties, I fear. No, the duchess, though of extended years, has sufficient energies to keep the *ton* atip when she has such a one as Anastasia to work with." He turned his attention to Claude. "Come, Claude, finish the wine. I noted an inn as we passed through Brensloe. We shall return to the town and arrange to have a man occupy this place."

"So soon?" Stacey asked, dismay registering on her face.

"Indeed, so," he answered. "By the evening of the morrow you two ladies and myself shall, under the careful hands of Claude at the lines, be on our way to the city. It will give me much pleasure to deliver you to the duchess."

Cora's eyes had been on him. "Sir, you said the two of us. Am I to understand that I go with the girl?"

"It could hardly be done otherwise. Would you have me compromise the girl before my mother has opportunity to enjoy her? Of course, you shall come. It strikes me that you have long been as mother to Anastasia. She will need the hand of reassurance ofttimes from someone she finds comfort with. Now, it is time. Prepare yourselves to remove to London." His glance fell on Stacey. "You view the situation as unfortunate at this moment, Anastasia. I feel you will think better of it within the matter of a few days in the whirl of my mother's London."

She attempted to force the expression of defeat from her face and replace it with a smile. "If I were certain of such a thing, my leaving this place would be greatly eased," she said sadly. "Is there no way I can remain here?"

"None," he said, getting to his feet. "Come, Claude, there is much to be done and little time to do it." He bowed to the two ladies. "Your good health, ladies. We shall return with a man to see to this place." He smiled down at Stacey and added, "I shall endeavor to choose one capable of seeing to the beauty of this farm as you have done, Anastasia. Concern yourself not."

She nodded, her glance going to Cora. "Very well, sir. It would seem our fathers have placed my future in the hands of you and your mother. I would only ask that, should I marry, I might be allowed to return here with my husband and Cora to take up the working of the place again."

A chuckle escaped the duke's lips. "Done," he said. "Though I wager within the matter of thirty days you will have little or no desire to return to this place. Mother will, unless I misguess, see to crowding your thoughts with other things." He bowed again. "We shall return as soon as arrangements can be made. Claude, let us go." Turning, he led the way from the house, leaving two confused females in his wake.

CHAPTER FIVE

Stacey was up at dawn of the fated day she was to be taken from her home. Quietly, lest she wake the still-sleeping Cora, she made her way from the house and began a circuit of the grounds in the newborn light of coming day. Tears filled her eyes and paths of silver traced her cheeks when she again entered the house and stepped toward the kitchen.

"Why, Stacey lass," Cora exclaimed as the girl entered the kitchen, "I assumed you to be still abed. What is the cause of your tears?"

Stacey sank into a chair and wiped at her eyes with a fist. "It is the knowledge that all I have strived toward over the last seven years does this day fall into the keeping of another," she said. "I feel tears shall come whenever my mind draws up memory of all this."

"There now, lass," Cora soothed, placing an

arm over the girl's shoulders. "Your years are too few for you to be so taken. I have spent the early hours considering the statements of the duke. I believe he has the way of it. There will be many things to crowd the memory of this place from your mind. Come, lass, smile. Consider ours an adventure to be enjoyed."

"It is an adventure I could well omit from my life," Stacey answered. Then she shrugged and stood. "There is nothing to be done for it. We must gather our belongings and make our way to the city with this duke." She shook the sympathetic hand from her shoulder and faced Cora squarely. "Very well, then, I shall play my role in this adventure. Come, let us prepare to take our leave."

The older woman studied her for a long moment before saying, "What have you in mind, lass? Is it something which will bring the ire of the duke upon you?"

Stacey smiled a tight-lipped smile. "The old woman, this duchess, wishes to play dolls with me, does she? Well, I shall convince her otherwise. I have no intention of allowing a hag in her dotage to make shambles of my life."

"You have not made the woman's acquaintance," Cora protested, unnerved by the anger apparent in the girl's expression. "Judge her not until the moment comes."

"What can she be but possessive of everything about her. She would add me to her ornaments and relive her youth through my being. I shall have much to say of that."

54

"Ah, Stacey," the abigail said sadly, "you allow your feelings for this place and the recent passing of your father to color your judgment. Pray, hold your anger until you are certain of the basis for your fears."

Tight-lipped, the girl turned from her toward her chambers. "We must prepare ourselves to leave, Cora," she said over her shoulder. "It would not do to keep this duke waiting. He might once again release his unfeeling wit upon us."

With a shake of her head the older woman followed the girl and assisted with the packing. They spoke little during the process. When all had been prepared in the girl's room, Cora said, "I shall complete my preparations. I see little value in removing any of the cooking utensils from here. Only our personal belongings will matter in the end."

"True," Stacey said, "for it will be only a short time before we are again at our ease in this, our home."

Cora swung to face her. "What is it, lass? What plan has taken shape in your mind?"

A bitter chuckle escaped the girl's lips. "Why, Cora, the terms of our going are plain, are they not? The duke himself has given his word that upon my marriage I shall be allowed to return to this place to live as I wish."

"And so?"

"We shall return soon, Cora. Fear not. There is little of London's dust which will settle on us."

"Oh, by the saints!" Cora exclaimed. "You cannot intend what you suggest, lass."

"I mean to fulfill the terms of my father's agreement," the girl interrupted. "There was no mention made of whom I should marry."

"But a season takes . . ."

"Season? I care not for a season. If marriage is required for me to remain here, then I certainly shall marry at the first opportunity. We shall not reside long in London, Cora. I will see to it."

Cora's features hardened. "Stacey, what you suggest is unworthy of you. Think, girl. The duke and the duchess offer you that which any in their right mind would give their all for. Do not injure yourself simply for a return to this property."

The girl's features remained frozen. "The duke will expect us to be ready when he returns, Cora. Let us not discuss this further."

"The packing is all but seen to," Cora answered, a suggestion of fear in her voice. "I beg you, Stacey, consider what you mean to do before taking steps which cannot be retraced."

At the woman's tone of concern the girl's expression softened. "You may rest assured, I will consider what is best for the both of us before taking step in any direction, Cora. Come, now, we must see to the preparations."

It was midafternoon before the duke's carriage drew to a stop at the gate. Stacey moved to open the door and stood waiting until Nigel had stepped from the coach and entered the gate. Then, dropping into a curtsy, she said, "Your grace, we are prepared to leave."

Nigel stopped in his tracks, his eye studying the

girl at his feet. "What are you about, Anastasia?" he asked, an expression of confusion on his features. "Has the night seen to the flying of your wits?" He bent to take her upper arms and bring her to her feet. "What is this charade you perform?"

His touch on her arms sent a strange feeling through her system. She met his glance, and for a moment she could not catch her breath. Then he released her and stepped back, asking, "Is it a method you have devised for repaying my sham of yesterday?"

"Sham, your grace," she said, aware of the color rising to her cheeks. "I hardly think one such as yourself could be accused of sham by one of my station, sir."

"Oh, dear God," he exclaimed, a hand going to his forehead. "Dear girl, your sarcasm is lost on me. I believe my mother shall have her hands full with the care of you. Enough of this." He turned to Claude. "See to their belongings, Claude. The hour grows late. I would see the last of Brensloe long before darkness makes itself known."

Cora arrived at the door at that moment. She stopped, her glance going from the duke to Stacey. Then exhaling heavily, she asked, "Is something amiss?"

Nigel nodded, a smile fixed on his lips. "It seems our lovely Anastasia has determined to make our trip to London a tense one, Cora."

The abigail's glance settled on the girl. "Stacey, it is not a point of breeding for you to act in such a manner. The duke does only what is required of him by his father's wishes."

"And I do nothing more than show proper respect for his position," Stacey answered. "By his own words his mother, the duchess, is concerned with his lack of interest in titles and responsibilities. I would show all their proper respect."

A tinge of color came into Nigel's face. "You try my senses, girl," he said. "What heinous crime have I committed that you are so disposed to barb me?"

Stacey sent a glance at Claude as he made his way into the house. Then returning her attention to Nigel, she said, "Crime, my lord? What possible crime could one of your station be accused of?"

Suddenly he snorted in humor. The icy smile became a warm one and he turned to Cora. "Is it possible the child assumes my so-called station allows all privileges?"

Cora could only nod. Confusion rode her features as she sent glances from one to the other.

"Well, then," Nigel said, adjusting the eye patch and moving a step closer to Stacey, "I shall exercise my powers by applying flat of hand to this spoiled child's hindside." He reached to clutch her upper arm and pulled her to him. "I assume your chemise is of such thickness to make a spanking bearable, little girl."

Her eyes opened wide at the statement and the query. She attempted to pull away from him, color flooding into her cheeks to turn her a bright red. "Unhand me, sir," she cried as he dropped to a knee and pulled her down over the other. "I will not be so mistreated."

He laughed heartily and brought the flat of his hand down on her backside. She screamed, more in anger than in pain. Then the hand again met her person and she jerked against his hold. "Unhand me, you . . . you . . ."

". . . Duke of Essler, the almighty power over Anastasia the Loving," he finished for her, giving her another swat. The hand did not fall again. Instead he stood, bringing her to her feet before him. His hands held her by the shoulders, and he looked directly into her eyes. "Now, small child, Anastasia, there will be no more of such actions as you have displayed. Should they again occur, I will be pleased to again administer the proper amount of education to you to make them cease. Is that clear?"

Tears filled her eyes as she met his glance. For a moment it seemed she would scream at him. Then she nodded.

"Very well, then. We shall have a pleasant trip to London." He turned to Cora, who stood openmouthed staring at him. "Cora, be kind enough to close your mouth and take your ward inside and see to her dress. Unless my senses defy me, she is without chemise beneath her outer garb." He paused to study the embarrassed girl and added, "What others only hope to do with whalebone, you do with what God has seen fit to give you. Amazing." With that he turned away from her to step toward the carriage.

Behind him Stacey felt her cheeks grow even

warmer. His comment concerning her lack of undergarments left her speechless and feeling much like the little girl he had indicated with his speech. She turned her embarrassed glance upon Cora. "I . . . I hate him," she burst out. "Oh, I shall . . ."

"Yes, child," Cora said, moving forward to comfort her. "Though it is a dastardly thing he has done, I feel you have, in a way, bargained for it." There was the beginning of a smile on her face as she added, "He is correct in other respects, also. You have been too long in the country. The dress alone is not enough for a lady's attire, especially a lady who, I feel, is destined to have a duke's hand on her backside often."

Taken by embarrassed anger, Stacey could only growl at the suggestion. She turned and stamped through the door, nearly colliding with Claude. That person noted the expression on the young girl's features and wisely kept his silence. His glance went to the abigail as she followed the girl into the house.

"Will the large trunk be a part of it, m'lady?" he asked.

Cora nodded, the beginning of a smile pulling at her lips. "The major part, I believe. It does contain all the lass's attire. There is weight to it, though. You will be in the way of needing assistance to move it."

"And he shall have it, Cora," the duke said from the doorway. "Where has our small hellion taken herself?"

Cora smiled back at him. "She is, unless I miss

my guess, attempting to bring both her color and her anger under control, sir." Her features hardened in reproach. "It was an unseemly thing you did."

He chuckled. "Unseemly? A duke can do something unseemly? Ah, to find such information at my age is shocking." He sobered suddenly and asked, "With your knowledge of the lass, is she destined to detest all but life on this ground, Cora?"

She was thoughtful for a moment before shaking her head. "No, your grace. She is but a child in the ways of the world. With my knowledge of her, I would venture your earlier prediction to be accurate. The thirty days you estimated for a changing of her views should be ample. I feel the girl is destined for London and society. A pity it has taken so long a time to come about."

Nigel nodded, the smile returning to his face. "Mother will wish to speak to you, I'm sure. She will, of necessity, require information you have concerning your ward. I believe you and Mother will become allies in seeing to the care of Anastasia."

"It is my wish to please the duchess in all ways, sir. The lass believes her to be . . ." She reddened suddenly and brought a hand to her mouth.

"Yes, go on. What is it Anastasia believes the duchess to be?" he prodded.

"She only this morning convinced herself that the duchess is a, your pardon, m'lord, a hag in her dotage."

61

Laughter full and rich rolled from the duke's mouth. When, moments later, he caught his breath, he smiled at the fearful Cora. "She does, indeed, live in a world of fantasy. Ah well, Anastasia will be surprised upon meeting with the duchess." He turned to Claude. "We waste time, Claude. I will assist you with the large piece. Come."

"A moment, your grace," Cora asked. "I would assist the girl in her attire. It is her room which contains the large trunk."

He nodded and she hurried away to assist her ward. Stacey turned to face her when she stepped through the door. "And what now, Cora," she demanded. "Does that woman beater wish to once again assault my person?"

Cora's smile gave way to an expression of irritation. Moving closer to the girl, she said, "Your father would be more than disappointed in your actions, girl. Whatever the duke has given you in the way of punishment was justly deserved. Open your eyes that the light of truth may enter. The duke and the duchess wish only to help you."

"Help me?" the girl demanded, her breath coming in angry bursts. "To help me, he lays hands on me in the manner of a spoiled child. Yes, and did refer to me as such, too."

Cora nodded. "And so you are, child. And more's the pity, I am at fault in that. Both your father and I did care so that we allowed you your way too often. You must forgo your childish manner, lass. You are grown and a lady. Allow his grace to bring you to the point your birth deserves."

"I will . . ."

"You will now don chémise under your garment," Cora interrupted, her voice growing hard. "For, unless you, this moment, begin the part of an adult, I shall take myself from you and seek employment elsewhere."

Stacey's eyes widened at the threat. "You would do such a thing to me, Cora?" she asked.

"To prevent you from shredding the life which is your due, I would, lass. Is it possible you believe me to be uncaring where you are concerned? Do you believe I coul1 remain idle while you dismiss such opportunity as is presented?"

The girl's stubbornness broke. Her eyes filled, and she moved to the waiting arms of the abigail. "Ah, Cora, without you about, I would be nothing. You are correct. I am a child. I shall need your constant assistance to become a lady in so short a time."

"You must first don a chemise. The duke awaits with his man to remove the heavy trunk. Come, lass, dry your tears and let us be on our way."

Some thirty minutes later, with the baggage stowed atop the carriage, Stacey stepped from the house with a tear-filled backward glance. She stopped and turned for a final look at the place which had been her home for the extent of her life.

"You will see it again if you desire, Anastasia," Nigel said softly from behind her. He placed a gentle hand around her shoulders and turned her to face him. "I would be a friend to you if you would so allow, girl. There are occasions when an older brother can be of some value to a girl." His good eye sparkled with sincerity.

His touch on her brought about the sensation she was constantly in a quandary about. She wiped at her eyes and met his glance. A warmth swept over her suddenly, bringing color to her features. She dropped her glance, saying, "Cora has informed me that I am, indeed, a spoiled child, your grace. I would apologize for my actions toward you."

He chuckled. "And I for my actions toward you, though the act of punishment was any but unpleasant for me. I assume you are now with chemise?"

Her color deepened. Her head came up. "Becoming a lady requires such, Cora informs me. I will manage until time when both my chemises become rags."

Leading her to the carriage, he laughed at her words. "You shall have gowns and chemises beyond your needs or thoughts by the time the duchess has her way, lass. Concern yourself not about the requirements of becoming a lady. The qualities are in you from your birth. Now, into the carriage with you. A long, and I fear, a rather uncomfortable journey awaits us. We shall stop at an inn later in the evening to take our rest. Then we shall move onto London with all possible speed on the morrow."

As she settled herself on the seat of the carriage, Cora entered and took a place beside her. For a long moment she studied the girl. Then, with a glance toward the door, she asked in a low tone, "What was it the duke said to bring the color to your features in so strong a manner, lass? Has he borne insult to you?"

Stacey shook her head. "He asked of my chemise, Cora."

The abigail inhaled sharply. "He made further mention of it? It is, indeed, unseemly for one of his rank."

The beginning of a smile touched Stacey's lips. "Our duke cares little for the manners of the titled, I believe. He will say or ask anything that enters his mind." She blushed and added, "He wishes to be an older brother to me."

Something in her tone brought the abigail's sharp attention to her. "Is there something afoot I am not aware of, lass?"

Stacey was quiet for a long moment. Then she said, "I cannot explain, Cora. It is only that when he nears me or touches me, a not unpleasant warmth seems to capture my body. Could it truly be that I am infatuated by him?"

"He is handsome," Cora answered. "But there are many, I am sure, who would have his attentions on them. Set not your heart on that one, lass. The role of duchess is not to be yours."

The girl blushed heavily at the statement. "I thought not of such a thing, Cora. It was only the sensation created by his touch which bothered me. There would be little hope of his taking note of a little sister such as myself."

Whatever the abigail's response would have been was cut off by Nigel's entrance into the carriage. Taking his seat across from them, he drew the door shut and smiled. "And we are off. I look forward to presenting the two of you to the duchess. May the trip be short and reasonably comfortable."

Several hours later, with Brensloe well behind them, they drew to a stop at an inn. Stacey was amazed at the deferential treatment shown her as she accompanied the duke to face the innkeeper.

"Ah, your grace," the dwarf of a man exclaimed. "Your return to my establishment gladdens my heart." His eyes settled on Stacey, and he bowed slightly. "M'lady, welcome to my humble inn."

"We would have quarters," Nigel said. "Lady Griffith and her abigail require adjoining rooms if possible."

"Of course, your grace. Water for the bath will be prepared soon." He again bowed in the girl's direction. "If you will follow me, m'lady." He led off toward the upper floor of the inn and showed her to a room which, while sparsely furnished, lacked nothing for cleanliness. "It is my hope the quarters suit the duke's lady," he said.

She colored at the statement. "I am not the duke's lady, as you suggest, sir," she corrected him. "But I thank you. The room is entirely suitable." She turned at that moment to face Cora who had mounted the stairs with a small traveling bag in hand. "Ah, Cora, there is a room for you down the hall from my own. Water for a bath is being prepared."

The abigail nodded, studying the innkeeper for a moment. "I shall see to your toilette as soon as the trunk is made available, lass. The duke quenches his thirst at this moment. We are expected for the evening meal."

"I shall prepare myself to step into the warmth of the water, then," Stacey answered. "I would appear at my best."

With relief showing plainly on her face, the abigail said, "Your manner eases my fears, girl. Perhaps you shall become a lady without the assistance of the duke's palm."

A flush at the memory of the spanking colored the girl's face. She smiled at the older woman, saying, "Let us pray that such a thing is never again necessary. Go now, Cora, and see to your quarters. I shall prepare for the bath."

When Cora had followed the innkeeper down the hall, Stacey closed the door of her room and moved to sit on the edge of the bed to await the coming of the bath water. Her glance went around the room, and she thought of the reception paid her as companion to the duke. "It does impress one," she said aloud. Then added, with a tilt of her head, "The duke's lady. I, Anastasia Griffith, am to be known as 'lady' from this moment on." The words were said in some surprise. She sat contemplating her new position until a knock sounded on the door. "Enter," she called.

The innkeeper and Claude entered the room, carrying the trunk. She directed them to place it

67

at the foot of the bed and thanked them. "I would have the small valise, also," she added.

Claude nodded. "Yes, m'lady. The duke sends invitation to dine at your convenience."

She smiled at him. "Tell the duke I shall be happy to join him once I have bathed and prepared myself."

Cora stepped to the door at that moment followed by two young lads bearing a wooden tub of steaming water. When the tub had been placed in the center of the room and the men had left, she faced the girl, saying, "A second tub awaits me, lass. I shall assist you in removing your garments and seeing to your bath before I partake of the same."

Stacey laughed outright. "And, Cora, do you assume I have forgotten the method of undressing and bathing myself? What has affected you in such a manner?"

The older woman studied her silently for a moment before saying, "It had, indeed, not occurred to me of our change, lass. Not until the innkeeper did refer to you as m'lady in the manner he did, did our new stations register on me."

Stacey's smile was wide. "He called me the 'duke's lady,' Cora. Was any such thing ever to be imagined? But the new position you refer to is but one of your mind. Nothing with us has changed, nor shall it. You are still Cora and I am still Stacey. Now, go to your bath. I have not become an invalid because of an innkeeper's greeting."

Cora hesitated, then her face broke into a smile. She shook her head. "Ah, lass, may you never change your ways." She turned to the door. "I shall return shortly to assist you with your dressing."

Once the abigail had gone, Stacey slipped from her clothing and stepped into the welcome warmth of the water. Sliding down until only her knees and shoulders were free of the water, she laid her head back on the edge of the tub and closed her eyes, savoring the relief brought on by the liquid warmth. The water, coupled with the strain of the day, had its way with her. She drowsed, then napped.

She was awakened by a tap at the door of the room. Realizing she had slept more than the length of time it had taken Cora to bathe and return, she called out for the abigail to enter and hastily began soaping herself.

The door opened and her eyes lifted in apology to the governess. Those same eyes widened to their limits when Nigel stepped into the room, her small valise in hand.

"I have your . . ." he began, then he became aware of her. For a moment confusion was uppermost on his features. Then, as she exclaimed in embarrassment and slid her upper torso under the water, he laughed, averting his glance. "It would seem you are again without chemise, Anastasia. It causes one to wonder if it is an aversion with you."

"I . . . I thought you to be Cora," she got out. "I . . . You should not . . ."

He chuckled again, keeping his glance off her. "True, I should not." He bent to place the valise on the floor and turned. "My apologies, m'lady. I will take my leave now." The door was nearly closed behind him and relief was flooding over her when his voice came again, saying, "Such an attractive birthmark and in such a fetching position."

For a long moment after the door closed behind him, she sat puzzling over the words. Then suddenly, the beet red of embarrassment flooded over her and she straightened in the tub. Her eyes dropped to the small strawberry birthmark centered low between her breasts, and she moaned, lifting her eyes to the heavens. "Ah, I shall never again be able to face him. What must the duchess believe of me when this is known?"

A tap on the door interrupted her at that moment. "Stacey, lass," came the call.

"A moment, Cora," she called, wishing the color to flow out of her. Finally, at the abigail's second call, she answered, "Come, Cora. I am in the bath."

The moment the older woman entered the door, her eyes narrowed. She studied the girl in the tub for several seconds before asking, "And what is it that has turned you the hue of red wine, lass? Is it my presence which so bothers you?"

Stacey could only shake her head. She began soaping herself again and shortly submerged herself in the tub and then stood.

Cora stood silently until she handed a towel to the girl. Then, an expression of curiosity on her face, she asked, "Are you ailing, lass?"

The memory of the duke's laughter at the sight

of her flooded Stacey's thoughts. A tinge of anger entered her system and, toweling herself, she said, "His humor is misplaced if he is indeed a gentleman."

"Of whom do you speak, Stacey?" Cora asked, concern in her voice. "Why do you mumble in anger? Has something been amiss?"

Stacey faced her to say, "The duke and his wit are more than expected, Cora. His pleasure at the discomfort of others is ill-befitting any of his position."

The older woman was silent for a moment. "And," she asked, "am I to continue wondering what has brought you to this state, lass? Or do you intend to confide in me?"

The color, which had subsided, again flowed through her. "It seems there is much I must learn of being ladylike, Cora. I chanced to fall asleep in the tub and a knock occurred at the door. Waking and thinking it to be you, I called permission to enter. It was the duke, bringing my valise. I was . . ."

The sharp intake of breath from Cora stopped her. "He entered while you were in the bath?" the abigail demanded. "He was aware of your . . ."

Realizing that she'd said more than she intended, Stacey shook her head. "No, no, Cora. It was only my knees and my head which were visible from the water," she lied. "It was the surprise of his being there in your place which did affect me."

"He did immediately close the door and offer apology, did he not?"

"Oh, instantly," the girl compounded the lie. "It was to his blind eye's side I was when he entered. My surprised cry did prevent him from even turning to me with his uncovered eye. He dropped the valise and closed the door with apologies to my person."

The abigail's glance went to the valise which sat a full two steps into the room. Then, moving quickly, she took the towel from the girl's hand and began drying her. "We must make haste. Even now, the duke will be awaiting our company."

Relieved that the woman was to make no further comment but aware of her glance toward the valise, Stacey remained silent until the toweling was finished and her apparel donned. Then, as the two made ready to leave the room, she said, "I do believe the duke is becoming an older brother to me as he suggested, Cora. The feeling is not an ill one."

The statement earned her a curious glance from Cora as they left the room and descended the stairs.

Nigel sat in an enclosed booth, awaiting their arrival. He stood when they came to the table, his smile broad, his good eye alight with the gleam of mischief. "Lady Anastasia," he said with a slight bow, "the green of your dress matches that of your eyes and they, together, make your hair a thing of beauty." He paused, the smile increasing and added, "There are moments when a man wishes for the use of both eyes that he might view even more of what is available to sight."

His beginning compliment had eased her tension somewhat, but the closing words sent a wish for death through her body. Fumbling for words in her embarrassment, she nodded and refused to meet the dancing devil alive in his eye. "Your grace is too kind," she said, glancing at the abigail and noticing the knowing expression on that woman's face. Suddenly she knew she could not spend the time required for a meal in the presence of the man who was amply aware of her endowments. She forced her glance up to meet his, saying, "I find no hunger within my body, your grace. I feel I must lie down else I shall suffer from . . ."

"Nonsense," he said. "Sit. Your ill feeling is caused by a harsh trip and a lack of food. Sit."

Reluctantly she settled herself into a chair. A twinge from her stomach told her she was indeed famished, but she would gladly have gone without food if she could but have escaped the expression in his single eye. "As you wish, your grace," she muttered, refusing to meet his glance.

He chuckled shortly. "Come, come, Stacey. May I call you that as Cora does?"

She nodded. "Of course, your grace. As you will."

"Then you must from this moment on refer to me as Nigel. Any feeling you have for or against me and your changed position cannot have basis in fact. We are for all intents and purposes brother and sister, are we not?"

She turned to the abigail. "Cora, before we are

73

served, I would have private words with the duke."

Curiosity alive in her expression, Cora nodded. "Of course, lass. I shall repair to the far table." She made her way across the room.

Nigel raised a hand to the eye patch and smiled at her. "Ah, and what is it you have in mind saying to me that requires such privacy, Stacey?"

She forced her glance to settle on his face. Crimson filled her face as she said, "I first wish to apologize for my actions earlier concerning the forced leaving of my home. It was unladylike of me, to say the least."

"Such an apology has already been given and does not call for privacy such as this," he told her, the smile remaining on his face.

She nodded. "I . . . I cannot think how to put words to what I wish to say. It does seem that my person is to hold few secrets from you in light of our recent meeting. I do not know how to express my feelings."

He chuckled. "You are thoroughly embarrassed that I should have seen you in the bath. Very well. That is as it should be. However, since I am in effect your protector and older brother, in spirit if not in fact, your embarrassment should be short-lived."

"It was your words as the door closed and again as I approached this table which caused the most embarrassment. A gentleman would never have allowed a lady to realize so completely that she had been observed."

74

The chuckle came again. The bare eye twinkled. "And?" he asked.

She had the feeling that she was talking herself into even deeper water. She met his smiling glance with reluctance. "And, I cannot meet the duchess, aware that she knows of such a thing. It is unseemly that Cora guesses more than anyone should. But your mother would think me a harlot or worse."

His chuckle became a laugh. "Ah, Stacey, do you seriously think I intend informing the duchess of what has occurred? Never. Gentleman I may not be, but I pray I am of more intelligence than to make common such knowledge of you as I have." He reached to tip her head up with a finger under her chin. "Forgive me for my taunting. I meant no insult to your person. Rather, indeed, the birthmark and all it protects is worthy of the most gracious compliments."

She inhaled sharply and pulled away from his touch. "You do it again, your grace. Must you forever refer to an occasion which was the fault of neither of us?" The thought crossed her mind that she'd done little except blush since the duke had come into her life. In the same thought she found herself pleased at his words concerning her appearance.

He sobered. "You are correct, little Anastasia. The devil is in me where you are concerned. But, to ease your mind, I have no designs on your body. True, God has blessed you with that which others spend fortunes to acquire. I do, however, have no interest in you other than as your protector. Does that ease the situation for you?"

For a moment she felt the desire to break into tears. His statement of lack of interest, instead of reassuring her, struck a painful chord in her breast. She finally nodded, saying, "If that is the way of it, I fear not for my safety, sir."

"Very well, then. May we now partake of some food? The night will be all too short, for we must rise early and be on our way if we are to arrive in London on the morrow."

Again she nodded. "Very well, your—"

"Nigel," he corrected. "Younger sisters only refer to older brothers by their given names."

"Very well, Nigel," she murmured. "My thanks for your assurances concerning what has taken place. I would hear no more concerning it."

He smiled at her. "And you shall not from me. Though I shall never forgive Napoleon for costing me the use of this accursed eye. The single one on occasion fills to overflowing."

Her glance came up swiftly at the words. "Oh ... You do try the saints, sir. I shall ..."

He reached to cover her hand with his own as she attempted to stand. An expression of true sorrow took his features. "I cannot imagine what there is about you that affects me so, Stacey. Truly I am sorry. I shall make every effort to control my words in the future. Now, please relax and let us speak of the matter no more."

She studied him for a long moment before saying, "Are you but having jest with me once again, sir? It would seem I am never to be free of your teasing."

The sober expression remained on his face. "On my word, girl, I have no intention of again bringing the blood of embarrassment to your features. I will control myself. Now, let us dine."

By the time the meal ended, Stacey was certain of his intent to live up to his word. She felt relief that she need not worry about his dropping an off-handed hint at her in the presence of the duchess or any other. She smiled to herself as she made ready for bed. "If London is destined to replace that which I have known," she said aloud, "then I must forgo the feelings brought on by this older brother of mine."

She sat thoughtfully on the edge of the bed for several minutes, wondering at her life within the same walls as the duke. Suddenly she smiled and slipped under the covers. "It cannot be any but interesting." She fell into sleep with the thought of her meeting with the duchess threading its way through her mind. "May she be as Nigel would lead me to believe," she told herself just before sleep overtook her.

CHAPTER SIX

It was midafternoon when the carriage turned into a flower-bordered drive and drew to a stop at the steps of a well-appointed town house. A liveried butler stepped from the house to open the carriage door and greet the duke.

Nigel stepped out and turned to hand Stacey down to the flagstone steps. He turned to indicate the house with a flourish. "Behold, the London base of the Essler Dukedom. Come, Mother will by now have been informed of our arrival. She will . . ." He broke off as the duchess stepped from the house and greeted him with a motherly hug.

She turned her attention from her son to study the girl, who stood as if fearing deadly peril. "So this is Anastasia Griffith," she said, her glance going back to her son. "A far cry from the scaly creature you expected, it would seem, Nigel." She extended her hands and took Stacey's. "Ah, your season shall be one to taunt the memories of all the *ton*, my dear. I am the Duchess of Essler. I knew your father. He was a good man."

Stacey dropped into a curtsy before the tall, gray-haired woman, saying, "He was, m'lady. My thanks for your concern in my behalf. I shall attempt to warrant your efforts."

A laugh escaped the woman's lips. "Come, come, child. It will not do for you to drop into curtsy each time we meet. You will, after all, be a part of this house. Stand so that I might see what it is my husband has committed to my care."

Embarrassed at the frank words, Stacey got her feet under her and stood silently while the duchess, dark eyes flashing, studied her from head to foot. Finally the older woman smiled and turned to her son. "A gem which needs only the slightest of polishing, Nigel. Don't you agree?"

Nigel laughed at the statement. "A gem in the rough, so to speak," he said. "There are edges and corners which have not become apparent to you, Mother. Though she is not the scaly creature I had imagined she would be, there are those . . ." He stopped, his glinting eye going to Stacey's face.

Stacey contained her anger only with the utmost effort. Finally she exhaled heavily, saying, "Your son does set his wit upon me at every turn, m'lady. It seems he does find me a ready door for the entrance of his humor."

"Indeed?" the duchess said, her curious glance going from the girl to the duke. "Then, lass, you have accomplished what none other has been able to since the end of the war. Until this moment Nigel has had little time for humor, no matter what the cause. If, indeed, he has shed his shell of concern about Napoleon, even for a moment, you have more than earned any consideration that is done for you in this house."

The words sent a thrill of pleasure through Stacey. She glanced at Nigel and noted a slight touch of color above his neckcloth. Then she turned her attention back to the duchess. "From his actions I would never have guessed him to be of serious mood, m'lady. It is my only salvation that he has stated his intention to become an older brother to me."

The expression on the duchess's features altered as she noticed the change in her son's eye. She nodded, saying, "Well, as older brother he should meet the requirements of any girl. Come, let us not spend the remaining portion of the day on the step. You are hungry, I am sure. There is food being prepared." She turned and led the way toward the house.

Behind the duchess Nigel moved close to Stacey and in a low voice, asked, "And is she the hag of dotage you expected, Stacey?"

Stacey turned an irritated glance on him. "She is lovely, sir." Her eyes widened suddenly. "You would not make mention of my earlier . . ."

He laughed outright, bringing the attention of the duchess back to them. "It would serve you well for your earlier actions toward me," he intoned. "Ah, well, it is the duty of older brothers to ever be available to assist the sisters in their deceptions. Fear not, little one. Your words are safe within my mind."

"Is there something I have missed?" the duchess asked.

"Only the introduction of Cora," he answered, "Stacey's abigail and confidante." He turned to indicate the governess who stood just outside the carriage.

"My years rob me of my senses," the duchess said. "I was so taken with the appearance of the young that I ignored the other." She nodded to Cora, adding, "I would have several moments of your time later in the day, Cora. There are those things which must, of necessity, require the both of us. Now, come, we shall have tea and await the serving of the meal."

Stacey felt the tenseness in her body as she stepped over the threshold of Essler House. Behind her the duke said, "Welcome, Stacey, to your new home. By the expression on my mother's face when she first beheld you, I would judge your stay here to be a short one. Within a sennight, I'm certain, she will have prepared you for the marriage market and within another of the same time, have handed you to one of the many swains who shall be pounding the paint from our door."

The duchess stood aside at the door of a dining room and smiled at Stacey. "Pay no attention to him, girl. He has little respect for what is required in the life of a lass such as yourself."

The tense feeling stayed with the girl through tea. When she'd finished, the duchess eyed her, saying, "Your trunk and valise have been taken to your rooms, Anastasia. A hot bath has been prepared and is waiting."

Stacey nodded, relieved that she could remove herself from the company for the moment to think her own thoughts. She was about to stand when the duchess turned her attention to Nigel.

"A post came for you only yesterday, Nigel," she said. "From France. Knowing you would more than likely return today, I did not send it on." She got to her feet and crossed to a small table to lift an envelope and hand it to him. "The perfume, like the handwriting, assures me that it is not from your enigma, Napoleon." She smiled at his frowning countenance as he accepted the missive and studied it.

Stacey watched the duke as he finally opened the letter and read it. She was aware of the change of expression on his features and wondered at the irritation he displayed.

The duchess, too, caught the change in her son. "Bad news, Nigel?" she asked.

His glance met hers and he shook his head. "Only a surprise I in no way expected, Mother. It seems we shall have a caller within the matter of a few days."

"A caller? And who, might I ask, is it to be?"

"A lady of my acquaintance from Paris," he answered. "Madame Colette DuBois by name."

The duchess studied him thoughtfully. "And from your frown at the knowledge that she is to make an appearance, I take it you are not pleased with her coming here."

He shrugged. "I had thought never to see her again once Napoleon was beaten. She served as an informant during my tour."

"I see," his mother said. She cast a glance at Stacey, hesitated at the expression on the girl's face, and finally said, "Anastasia, your trip must have tired you. The bath water would surely ease you. Go, child. I must speak with the duke."

Stacey, the words jerking her back from her thoughts, stood. "Yes, m'lady, you are correct. A bath will help remove the dust of the trip and the tenseness of my body."

The duchess crossed to a bell cord and, a moment later, a maid entered the room to show the girl to her quarters. When they were alone, the duchess faced her son, saying, "And now, Nigel, I would have information concerning both our new ward and this soldier friend of yours from France. Come, sit beside me and tell me of your trip to Brensloe."

He covered the details of his trip sketchily and ended by saying, "And so, we have arrived with Miss Griffith in tow, as it were. I do believe you shall find her to be more than a handful, Mother. She is, when she makes her mind up, devilishly hard to convince."

"And you have told what you wish me to know. Now, my son, tell the rest. What is there that has happened that brings the color to the girl's face when she meets your eye? Have you in some way become privy to something to which you are not entitled concerning her?"

His glance dropped from hers. He reached to adjust the eye patch. "I can't imagine where you gain such thoughts, Mother. It is true, I do find myself pestering her in many ways. But I have assured her that I shall cease. Other than that, there has been nothing."

"From her expressions since entering this house, it would seem she is taken with you somewhat. She is at an impressionable position in her life, only recently being from the farm."

His glance came up to meet hers. "She is as a younger sister to me. She mentioned the fact earlier, you will recall."

The duchess nodded. "I recall. She would not be the first sister to find infatuation in an older stepbrother."

He laughed. "The suggestion is absurd, Mother. If anything, she hates me or at least did for some moments. We are at present involved in a truce with one another. No, there is nothing like what you suggest."

She nodded without commenting further on the subject. When she again spoke, it was to ask, "And this Madame Colette. Was she a close acquaintance of yours in Paris?"

He nodded. "She was. She is a wonderful woman, though different than any in London. You will meet her within two days according to her letter."

"Was she a very close acquaintance?"

For a moment he faced her as if there would be no answer. Finally he nodded. "Yes, Mother, she was a very close acquaintance. It was in me to seek her hand once the war was finished. It did, however, pass from my thoughts amid the demands of the duchy."

"If you felt for her in such a way, what reason could you have for the intense frown brought on by the news of her coming. It seems the odd part for a lover."

He hesitated a moment, then with a shrug, said, "It is only that there is no reason for her coming. It can only cause gossip. You are aware of the tales which fly with any French lady's arrival at this time. I would not have such tales to bear at this moment. There is much to be seen to in my duties as Duke of Essler."

"And do you still love her?"

Again he shrugged. "If ever I did, I still do. I had not thought of her for some time. Why do you ask?"

The duchess straightened and met his uncovered eye with a straightforward glance. "Had it not occurred to you that she comes to London to rekindle the relationship begun in France?"

He nodded. "It has occurred to me. I cannot tell you how I will react to such a thing if, indeed, it happens. We shall have to bide our time and see, shall we not?"

"It is, I suppose, the only way. Well, look well to your heart, my son. The duties of a duchess are demanding. Be certain your chosen is of the quality to bear them."

He chuckled suddenly. "You would have me

wed before I am aware of my feelings, Mother. Do not concern yourself on that score. Perhaps the visit from Colette is nothing more than her desire to see London and spend a holiday in the markets."

"Perhaps," his mother agreed. "Well, we shall wait and see. Meanwhile I would speak with the girl's abigail. What was her name?"

"Cora," he answered, getting to his feet. "You will find that one dedicated to Stacey in the manner of a staunch defender."

"And so must we all be, for she is of the Essler blood, no matter how far removed." She took on a pleased, thoughtful expression at the mention of the girl. "Ah, she will send the tongues of the *ton* wagging on her first appearance. I foresee a steady swirl of swains bargaining for her favors. It will again be like years past when the Esslers were the toast of London."

He smiled at her schemes. "May Almack's and the biddies there prepare themselves for war."

"You are much like your father," she said, the beginning of a smile at the corners of her mouth. "And as Duke of Essler, you will be required to take the portion of saying 'Aye' or 'Nay' to potential suitors of your claimed younger sister. Had you prepared yourself for such a thing?"

He looked down at her, an expression of distaste on his face. "I? What right have I to choose a suitor for Stacey? She is in her twentieth year and lovely beyond imagining for a child of those years. Sorting through the parcel of young swains she will attract will require the times of the ages."

She smiled broadly at the statement. "What you say is true. You will, however, need only to choose those of your liking. Once that is done, the rest will of necessity be restrained until the moment it is known whether a match is truly made."

"The duty should be that of the duchess, I should think," he argued. "How am I to know which is her preference?"

The duchess shook her head in a suggestive manner. "Her preference is important. What is more important is that she does not come afoul of the rakes who are only too abundant within the bounds of London. You, as a man and the duke, recognize many of those who are unsuitable for any girl. It is your duty to see that she chooses wisely."

"Drat!" he exclaimed. "Do you tell me Father allowed himself to be placed in such a position?"

"The occasion never arose," she answered. "But there were many times when your father took upon himself unpleasant chores as his duties required. Come, my son, it will require nothing more than a nod from you. You shall do beautifully." She stood and reached to pat him on the cheek. "Now, I would speak with this Cora of her ward. Do what you will with the rest of the day and think on the preparations you wish made for the arrival of Colette."

Turning to leave her, he said, "I see no reason for special preparations. She will arrive and leave. I shall see that Cora is sent to you." He left her there.

As her son stepped from the room, the duchess stood frowning. Finally she shook her head in confusion and said aloud, "Ah, Nigel, I hope you do not betake fascination for love. For there is nothing of love for this Frenchwoman in your feelings." Her thoughts were still on the duke when Cora entered the room moments later and dropped to curtsy before her.

"Your grace," the abigail said, "you wished to speak with me?"

"Yes," the duchess said. "Come, sit beside me. I would know all of your Anastasia. Is she of flighty mind and eye?"

"Oh no, m'lady," Cora answered, taking a seat beside the older woman. "She is but a child in spirit, though of an age where such is unexpected. She has been protected from much that others take as their usual helping of life. It is unfortunate at times."

"But helpful in that it leaves the hue of innocence within her when others have lost it years earlier. Tell me, is she in love with the duke?"

Cora's eyes widened, her mouth dropped, and she stuttered, "I ... I ..."

"Come, come," the duchess said, "there is much to be read in the eyes of a girl of her years. You know her as well as any. Is she in love with my son?"

Cora shook her head in confusion. "I know not, m'lady. She does seem infatuated past the point of mere friendship with his grace. They, the two of them, do act as brother and sister at times.

89

There is the matter of . . ." She paused, dropping her glance. "But that is of no concern," she said.

"You were about to speak of some matter concerning the girl and my son. What is it?" the duchess asked.

"It was nothing, m'lady. Only an incident which occurred at the inn on the evening last. It is of no import, I'm told."

"But you do not so believe. Tell me of the incident and of your feelings toward it."

Cora hesitated a moment, then under the understanding eye of the duchess, said, "It seems the duke did enter Stacey's room while she was in the bath. It was not done intentionally, I assure you. And the girl assures me that he did immediately remove himself upon learning that she was in such a state. It was with his covered eye toward her that he entered the room, I'm told."

"And you believe what?" the duchess asked, her voice low.

Cora shrugged. "I entered only shortly after, m'lady. The valise which the duke had brought to Stacey sat easily two steps within the room. I hardly believe his grace could have placed it there without taking note of the girl in her bare state."

Suddenly the duchess chuckled. "And has the duke made reference to the incident in any way since then?"

Cora colored. "He did at the time of the evening meal make comment that he ofttimes wished for the use of both eyes to be able to view more of what was within sight. The statement did bring the color of heavy embarrassment to Stacey's features."

"Ah," the duchess sighed. "Though it sounds ill of me, Cora, I am glad to hear this. I rejoiced within when the girl mentioned the manner in which my son had been teasing her. This affair, though serious to be sure, relieves me as well. It is a good sign that he teases her in such manner. He has been too long involved with the serious concerns of Napoleon."

"Yes, m'lady," Cora answered, obviously not completely understanding. "Will there be anything else, m'lady?"

"There will, indeed. Anastasia must be fitted as is her due to face the approaching season. Even now, the city is becoming crowded with those who are to make their first appearance. The materials are in short supply. We must begin immediately to acquire the gowns necessary for her. A hairdresser must be employed. My own will not do for he is too fastidious for the young. Yes, there is much to do and it will be our lot to see to it."

Cora stood. "Oh, m'lady, if I could but express my feelings at what you do for the child. It is beyond compare. I shall inform her of the need for haste in matters."

The duchess waved a hand. "There is no need to excite her beyond the point of common sense. Morning will serve well enough as a starting hour for us." An expression of dreaminess cloaked her eyes. "She will be the toast of London or I miss my guess."

Cora's eyes shone with anticipation. "Ah, to see the lass, who is as daughter to me, allowed such a season as you describe does send the blood rushing through my senses, m'lady. Might I be allowed permission to attend both yourself and Stacey on the visits to the clothiers?"

The duchess smiled at her. "Of course, Cora, for there are those things you will need also. The abigail of the duke's younger sister can hardly appear in public in less than fine wear."

"Me, m'lady? I have all the . . ."

"Nonsense. You love the child. To keep you from the edges of the parties and galas she will surely attend would be criminal. It is the sight of a loved one becoming accomplished that is the greatest pleasure to parent or guardian. You shall be a part and parcel of the season."

"Yes, m'lady," Cora got out amid her obvious excitement. "And thank you, m'lady."

"Now, we must, at the earliest on the morrow, take ourselves to the city. See that the lass is ready."

"Yes, m'lady," Cora said, turning to leave.

"And, Cora," the duchess said as the abigail was about to step from the room.

"Yes, m'lady?"

"If you sense or learn of the girl's true feelings toward my son, I would know of it."

"Yes, m'lady," Cora answered.

When she'd gone, the duchess sat back and sighed thoughtfully. He could do worse, she told herself, a half smile riding her lips. Yes, he could do much worse.

CHAPTER SEVEN

Stacey was removing herself from the bath when Cora entered the room. The girl faced her, wrapped in a luxurious towel bearing the Essler coat of arms. "Is not all of it too much to believe, Cora?" she asked.

Cora smiled at the girl, seeing the pleasure in her eyes. "Aye, it is that, lass. You must dress yourself for the duchess. I feel she will wish to speak with you shortly. I have only this moment left her."

An expression of fear captured the girl's features. "And is she satisfied with me, Cora? Does she consider me worthy of her efforts?"

The abigail laughed. "Is this the same young one who only two days ago was so scornful of all having to do with the duchess and with London?"

Stacey colored at the reminder. "Ah, Cora, I had no idea it could be as it is. The duchess is a delightful lady. The duke, while trying at times, seems to be the finest of men. The acceptance afforded me by the both of them is beyond my belief. I feel as if I shall burst with happiness."

"And of your desire to return to the farm, lass?"

Stacey sobered. "I still would return there, Cora. Though, it is to be admitted, I wish to partake of all possible before such a return. The duke gave his word to me that my return would be allowed. There is no urgency."

Cora nodded understandingly, a smile on her face. "Then you shall not take the first available suitor as your spouse?"

Stacey laughed at the question. "Ah, it was but a childish thought mentioned in anger at imagined wrongs done me, Cora. No. I shall not hurry to wed." She donned a robe and repeated the question, "What of the duchess's thoughts concerning me, Cora? What has she said?"

Cora repeated the plans laid forth by the duchess for the preparations for the girl's coming out. When she had finished, Stacey's eyes burned with excitement.

"Oh, we shall have such fun, Cora. Did she say anything of me? Of my manner? Oh, I would please her if I could."

"You need have no worry along those lines, lass," the abigail assured her. "She did ask if your feelings toward the duke were beyond the norm."

"She asked that?" Stacey asked in surprise. "For what reason? Does she imagine I have set my cap for her son?"

"No, lass. She simply imagined something in

your glances toward him. She wished to know the truth of things as I saw them."

"And you told her what, Cora?"

Cora shrugged. "That I thought you to be . . ." She was interrupted by the sounds of a carriage drawing to a stop at the front of the house. Crossing to the window, she looked down to see a lady in a plumed hat step from the carriage and approach the door of the house. Turning back to the girl, she said, "Enough of this talk. It seems a visitor has arrived. You will be expected to be present for introduction unless I miss my guess. Come, you must dress quickly."

"Was it a gentleman?" Stacey asked, shedding the robe and allowing the abigail to assist her in her dressing.

"Gentlemen seldom wear plumed hats of the nature I noted from the window. It was a lady. A wealthy one by her dress."

Memory of the message received by Nigel swept through the girl's mind. "Oh, could it perhaps be the Frenchwoman, Cora?"

"I know of no Frenchwoman, lass. But for that matter, it could be the queen. I know not. If you will but remain still for a moment, I will do as I can with your hair and you will be able to discover who it is."

When the abigail completed her efforts with the hair, Stacey made her way downstairs to the drawing room. She was about to enter when she became aware of a low, sultry feminine voice saying, "Ah, chéri, to be within the circle of your arms again is as an entrance to heaven itself. Kiss

97

me, chéri." A silence followed the words, a silence which Stacey found unbearable. Then the duke's voice said, "But, Colette, your letter placed you here two days hence. Nothing has been done in the way of preparations."

"And none are needed, chéri. To be near you is enough. Had you forgotten Colette entirely?"

"It is something I could never do, you know. No, the dukedom and my other duties have had their way with my time."

Stacey forced herself forward. She entered the room and felt a physical pain in her bosom at the sight of a lovely dark-haired woman in Nigel's arms. She coughed slightly into her hand, bringing their attention to her.

"Ah, Stacey," Nigel said, releasing his hold on the woman to come toward the girl. "Come here, girl. I would have you meet Madame Colette DuBois of Paris. She is an old friend and a valuable one."

Stacey allowed herself to be led forward. She dropped into a partial curtsy before the older woman, her eyes on the floor. "I am pleased to make your acquaintance, m'lady," she said.

The Frenchwoman chuckled. "Ah, Nigel, and what is this you have? A child by a secret marriage?"

"Hardly," Nigel answered. "Few men become fathers at age seven. Stacey is the daughter of a close friend of my departed father. She prepares for her season beginning tomorrow. She is as a younger sister to me, aren't you, Stacey?"

The words brought sudden rage to the girl's

senses. Realizing her color was high, she endeavored to control herself enough to say, "As you wish, Nigel."

The woman laughed, a soft, tinkling sound in the expanse of the room. "And a very lovely little sister she is, Nigel. She shall have all the young men at her feet."

"I suspect you are correct. But come, seat yourself. Tea will be here shortly. Tell me, what brings you from Paris at this time?"

The woman turned away, ignoring the girl. "Must one have a reason to call on old friends, Nigel? Is it not enough that I wished to see you? Most men would be flattered by such devotion."

"And so I am," Nigel assured her, standing till both she and Stacey had taken seats. "It is only that my duties will leave me little enough time for you."

"Ah, yes, your dukedom must be seen to. Also, I am informed, you are the most important of all the advisors as to the affairs concerning Napoleon."

Nigel nodded. "I am a portion of the planning, yes. There is little enough to plan now that he is on his island. There are few who believe as I do that the man will never allow himself to be kept captive."

Colette laughed at this. "Ah, Nigel, my love, you worry where none is due. What can the little emperor do from his island? England wastes her resources with concern. The armies might as well be disbanded. Napoleon is beaten."

He looked at her for a long moment before saying, "Perhaps. And since the armies have indeed been disbanded, let us pray you are right."

The duchess entered the room at that moment, and Nigel got to his feet, saying, "Mother, may I present Madame Colette DuBois, a most vigorous worker for the revolutionaries of France."

The Frenchwoman curtsied slightly to the duchess, a smile on her face. "Your grace, Nigel has so often spoken of you. He is a son to be proud of."

The duchess met her glance squarely and nodded. "He is at times more than enough for any mother. You were involved directly with the revolution, madame?"

"Since the moment of my husband's death at the hands of Napoleon, your grace. It was little enough for me to do."

"Of course. Well, and where is the tea?"

"On its way, Mother," Nigel assured her as the women seated themselves.

The duchess put her attention on Stacey who sat quietly studying the Frenchwoman. "You have met our newly arrived Anastasia, have you not, Madame DuBois?"

"A lovely child," the woman answered, "with all of life ahead of her. Let us hope it will be a life more simple than that which I have known."

A smile tugged at the corners of the older woman's lips as she noted the fire in Stacey's eyes. She nodded. "Without the concerns of war, you mean?"

"Certainly," Madame DuBois answered. "There are few of the young ones today who could cope with matters such as were second nature to Nigel and myself."

"Ah, you do speak as if you are ancient, madame."

The Frenchwoman met the older woman's eyes and smiled. "It was not my intention to dismiss the young ones offhand, your grace. I meant simply that the easy life has been their portion. There is much afoot in the world which would rob them of their senses."

The duchess turned her glance to Nigel, who sat watching her and the newcomer with undisguised curiosity. "And, Nigel," she asked, "have arrangements been made for Madame DuBois to remain at the House of Essler?"

He straightened, his glance going to the Frenchwoman. "I assumed her plans were made, Mother." To Colette he added, "Are you yet quartered elsewhere, Colette?"

The plumed hat moved precariously as she shook her head. "Having a desire to again see you, I came straight here, Nigel. It is of no concern. There are several I may call upon for the necessities."

"Nonsense," the duchess interrupted. "You will reside with us for as long as you remain in London. The hand of a woman such as yourself will be a welcome asset in the preparation of Anastasia for her coming out. We shall make use of the obvious talents you are privy to in the manner of dress and hairstyles."

Madame DuBois nodded. "It would be my pleasure to assist the child. There is much which can be done to fashion the plain into the unique. It should prove amusing."

The duchess had been watching Stacey from the corner of her eye. Noting the anger building in that young face, she got to her feet, saying, "Yes. Well, we shall look forward to pleasant days during your visit." She turned to Stacey. "Anastasia, come with me. There is much we must speak of before our travels to the shops tomorrow."

Her young eyes flashing, Stacey got to her feet, and with a slight nod of her head to both the duke and the Frenchwoman, followed the duchess from the drawing room.

"We shall closet ourselves in my chambers, girl," the duchess said as they made their way through the huge house. "What I am to say to you is for your ears only."

Detecting a note of irritation in the woman's words, Stacey's thoughts left the Frenchwoman and the duke and fixed on what she had done to bring about the change in the manner of the duchess. "I have irritated you, m'lady?" she asked as the older woman opened a door and entered a splendid room done in pinks and whites.

Waving the girl to a settee, the duchess faced her, her features stern. "You have done nothing to irritate me, Anastasia. My irritation stems from your lack of knowledge in the ways of worldly women."

"M'lady?"

"Your expressions are too simple to read, girl. Your instant dislike of the Frenchwoman was as obvious as the fingers on my hand. You must not allow such a thing to happen again."

Stacey dropped her glance and said in a murmur, "She makes a point of calling me a child to the duke. I am in my twentieth year and hardly a child."

"Ah, but you are, lass," the duchess said, her tone softening. "In the ways of women such as Madame DuBois, you are the most innocent of all innocents."

Stacey brought her glance up, asking, "You suggest she is not a lady?"

"I suggest no such thing. She is obviously the widow of some wealthy Frenchman who lost his life in one way or another. She is, however, a woman of much knowledge which will never be your misfortune to know."

Anger formed the lines of Stacey's face into rigid seams. "She called me plain, m'lady. Even children do not choose to be so labeled."

A chuckle escaped the lips of the duchess. "Ah, Anastasia, could you not see what she was about?"

Confusion swept over the girl's face. "I do not understand your meaning, m'lady."

Crossing the room to sit beside the girl, the duchess lifted one of her hands and patted it. "Ah, there is so much you do not know of life. The woman sensed immediately that you were a contender for Nigel's feelings. Weren't you aware of her instant antagonism?"

Stacey nodded. "She hated me on first sight, I knew that. But for her to believe that I have . . ."

"Be not too sudden with your declarations, Anastasia," the older woman warned. "As I have said, your feelings are as readable as the penny post. There is an expression in your eyes when you face Nigel which, while it may not be, was mistaken for an interest in him. That is the reason for Madame DuBois's acid tongue where you are concerned."

"She is old," Stacey said.

"She is not," the duchess corrected. "She has more years than she will admit to, I'm sure, but she is not old. She is attractive to men as only a woman who makes men a study can be."

"You are suggesting she is immoral?" Stacey asked, shocked. "She is a widow of a Frenchman of wealth, you yourself said so."

"French widows with titles come in quantities unbelievable, Anastasia. Titles in France are as frequent as potatoes in a market. She is not the question, however."

"I beg your pardon, m'lady. I misunderstand your meaning."

"Your thoughts and intentions are of concern to me at this moment. Tomorrow you begin your preparations for a season which promises to be the finest in the history of London. Will you, from the outset, have your mind set on a choice in spite of all who are bound to seek your favors?"

"A choice? I know none to make choice from at this moment, m'lady."

The duchess sighed. "I wonder if you misunderstand my meaning by choice, girl? Very well, then, I shall be direct. Have you set your heart on wedding the duke?"

Stacey's mouth dropped open. "The duke! I am but a little sister to him, your grace. He would as leave . . ."

"I asked not of his feelings, but of yours."

Confusion took the girl. She shook her head, saying, "I cannot think how to answer you, m'lady. I am but hours in your acquaintance. I . . ."

"It takes only moments to form sympathies which last a lifetime, Anastasia. I intend no disfavor if your feelings for my son are as I suggest. It would, in fact, bear some consideration on the parts of both you and him. However, if you are so inclined, you must realize that many have thrown themselves in Nigel's sight, and he has had time for none of them. Madame DuBois is an old and close acquaintance from France. She is different from the others in that a certain intimacy has grown between her and my son. You will need all your wits about you when she is in your company. Otherwise you will appear as the child she calls you."

Stacey sat silently for a long moment before saying, "My senses do deceive me, m'lady. It appears to me that you wish to assist me in gaining your son as suitor. You have known me less than a day's time. I cannot understand such a thing."

"You are the daughter of one I knew well, Anastasia. There is much of him in you, I've already determined. Though I would force none on

Nigel, I would have him aware that there are others besides Madame DuBois. I speak so now only because of the obvious haste she makes toward endearing the duke to her."

"You believe she wishes to become the Duchess of Essler, m'lady?"

The duchess chuckled bitterly. "Can there be any question of it, Anastasia? Think you she came this distance only to see the shops of London and to say hello to an old friend? No, the woman has plans. One of those plans, without doubt, is the attainment of the title of duchess for herself. She will be a worthy foe for my talents."

Stacey shook her head in confusion. "I must truly be the innocent you say, m'lady. You have invited her to assist in the choice of my gowns and my hair arrangement. I would trust her not at all with anything to do with my person."

The chuckle came again, though not bitterly. "Ah, lass, if we but use our given wits, the DuBois woman will, indeed, tell us exactly what will be to your best advantage. Allow me to see to that. Now, tell me of yourself. Do you sit the saddle well? Is the pain of your father's death past? Tell whatever it is that you consider important of yourself."

Stacey shrugged. "I sit saddle as well as any who has ridden since age four, I suppose. And the sting of my father's passing, while still acute, has eased. He is yet in my thoughts on many occasions."

"Which is as it should be. He was, indeed, a

fine man and a true one," the duchess said, an expression of thoughtfulness in her eyes.

"You spoke of knowing my father well, m'lady. Were you friends?"

"Ah, yes," was the answer. "We were the best of friends." She fixed the girl with a steady glance. "Were you aware that your father saved the duke's life on two occasions?"

Stacey shook her head. "No, m'lady. No mention had been made of it by Father."

The duchess nodded. "So like him. His accomplishments were as nothing to him. I would have you know, for your own information and no one else's, that your father and I were at one time promised. No, don't look at me in such surprise. I felt very deeply for your father. It was only upon meeting the late duke that I realized my deeper feelings belonged to another."

Stacey sat with open mouth at the disclosure. Finally she said, "Your words explain much that has confused me, m'lady."

The duchess nodded. "Yes, your father was a wonderful man. He was the best friend either the duke or myself could claim. And your mother, who became wife to your father two years after my marriage to the duke, was equally wonderful. You come from the best of stock, Anastasia. Let no one convince you otherwise. Now we must prepare for dinner. I would advise you in the manner of your dress if it will not come as an insult to you."

"Certainly not, m'lady," Stacey exclaimed. "It is

your house. I would learn the manners of your household."

The older woman waved a hand in deprecation. "I spoke not of the manners of the house, girl. I spoke of our intent to prevent the Frenchwoman from seeing a completion of her plans where Nigel is concerned."

Stacey's glance dropped. "I doubt that I will be able to equal the dress of the woman with my meager clothing, m'lady. I cannot hope to impress any when she is about."

"Enough of such talk, girl," the duchess snapped. "Come, we shall go to your chambers and view that which is available." So saying, she led the way from her room down the hall to the chambers which had been given Anastasia.

Entering the room, she fixed the abigail with a stern glance. "Cora, I would have the gowns of the child laid out. We must attire her for dinner."

Cora looked at her in confusion. "Gowns, m'lady? You refer to the finery of the courts? She has no such thing, only the simple dresses needed by the women of the farm communities."

"Then they will have to do for the moment. I would see them."

Cora moved quickly to do as the duchess bade. When the eight garments were displayed on the bed, the countess moved around them in deep thought. Finally she pointed to a simple dress of pure white with a high neck and long sleeves. "That one," she pronounced. "Anastasia, don the garment and let us see how you appear. I shall return momentarily. I must see to the comfort of our new guest and advise the servants of the number for dinner." She swept from the room, leaving the girl and the abigail staring at each other in wonder.

CHAPTER EIGHT

"What is afoot, Stacey lass?" Cora asked when the door closed behind the duchess.

Stacey shook her head in sorrow. "Ah, Cora, the Frenchwoman I mentioned earlier is even now invited to remain at Essler House for her stay in London. The duchess takes my part in a hatred that sprung between the woman and myself at first sight. I do not understand, but I shall allow her to guide me."

Cora nodded. "For whatever the reason, your decision is a good one. The duchess appears wise beyond any I have known. Come. Don the dress and tell me all that has happened."

Getting into the dress and repairing her hair, Stacey repeated the tale of her meeting with the Frenchwoman and the ensuing events. "I know not what the duchess has in her mind, but she does feel I am to be the means of spiking the guns of this Frenchwoman, Cora."

"And she was not opposed to your preference for the duke?" Cora asked as she buttoned the dress at the back.

Stacey turned to face her. "My preference for the duke? You talk as if I had indeed set my cap for him, Cora. I assure you, he would see nothing of me in such manner even if it were my desire to be so taken."

The abigail nodded. "As you say, Stacey. Now, turn around and allow me to finish the fastening of your dress. The duchess will return shortly and wish to view you."

The words had hardly left her mouth when the duchess reentered the room, saying, "Nigel has already seen to the woman's comfort. She is even now preparing for dinner." She stopped, her glance going from Stacey's head to her feet and back again. She nodded. "Excellent. I believe this will be the very thing."

Stacey curtsied, saying, "Thank you, your grace. I hope I will not be a disappointment to you."

The older woman snorted in humor. "Your appearance is that of the innocent you are, Anastasia. There is nothing the Frenchwoman can do to accomplish such an appearance. Yes, you will do nicely. Now, come. Dinner will be announced within a short time. I would be at the proper place when she makes her entrance."

In complete confusion Stacey followed the older woman from the room and down the stairs.

When they reached the ground floor, the duchess turned to her, saying, "Come, lass. You will wait in the library until the moment I come for you. I shall see to it that dinner is announced and await the entrance of Madame DuBois."

"I fail to see the meaning of all this, m'lady," Stacey said. "What is the purpose of my waiting in the library?"

The duchess shook her head. "There is no time for explanations of experienced women. Do as I tell you and you will realize the necessity for my decisions soon." She led the girl to the library and, as she was turning to leave, said, "If the door is left open a crack, you will have access to sight of the Frenchwoman as she descends the stairway." Then she was gone, leaving Stacey alone with her jumbled thoughts. She was back in minutes to say, "I have only now had dinner announced. Within a matter of ten minutes, when she assumes all to be present, she will make her way to the dining room. I shall come for you then." She again left Stacey alone.

Shortly after the duchess had taken her leave, Stacey moved to the door of the library to open it a crack. She stood in a position so that she could view the lower portion of the staircase and waited. Several minutes later the ruffled hem of a richly purple gown came into her view and she tensed. Seconds later she moaned softly in anguish as the full picture of the Frenchwoman came into sight. Ah, she is beautiful, she told herself as she viewed the low-cut bodice of the gown and the exquisite black hair piled high upon the woman's head. Then the DuBois woman passed from her view.

Stacey stood at the door feeling self-pity and anger when the duchess entered the library with a finger to her lips calling for silence. "In but a few moments you shall go to the dining hall, lass," she said. "I have told the French one you are remiss and that I would fetch you."

"Her beauty is beyond compare," Stacey said. "I shall appear as a wretch beside her."

The duchess chuckled. "The beauty of bottles cannot compare with God's own work, child. Concern yourself not."

"We wait for what, m'lady?"

"Why, I have told both her and Nigel that you are still in your room. Do you believe it possible for one of the age I am to traverse the stairs in so short a time? Wait. A few more minutes will serve for Nigel to fill his eyes with her. Then we shall make our entrance."

"Her gown does expose an ample bosom that could hardly go amiss in the duke's sight, m'lady. This simple dress makes me appear as nothing."

The duchess shook her head, a smile riding her lips. "Ah, Anastasia. The volumes of which you are ignorant concerning men is amazing. Come, it is time. Follow me and walk proudly."

"I shall try, your grace," Stacey answered, following the woman from the room. "But to what end, I cannot fathom."

The duchess remained silent until they had entered the dining room. Then, as she made her way to the foot of the table, opposite her son, she said,

114

"The girl was attempting to choose among the too few garments at her disposal. I pointed out that it was nothing but a family dinner. Any dress of the few would suffice."

Stacey was aware of the narrowing of the Frenchwoman's eyes as they scanned her. Then she gave her attention to the duke who had risen from his seat and was approaching her. There was no mistaking the appreciation apparent in the gleam of one eye. He neared her and took her hand to bend over it. The light brush of his lips on her skin was momentary, then he was looking directly into her face, a smile riding his lips. "And are you with chemise, sister Stacey?" he whispered for her ears only.

The instant color which invaded her face brought a chuckle to his lips. He turned to lead her to a seat on his left, directly across from the DuBois woman. Then, his amused glance still on her, he took his seat, saying, "Ah, for one such as myself to have the three most beautiful women of all Europe as dinner companions must indeed be a blessing of the duchy. Ladies." He lifted his wine cup in toast.

As Stacey lifted her cup, she was aware of the raw hatred visible in the glance of the Frenchwoman. She glanced at the duchess and saw an expression she did not understand on that face. Then the duke was speaking again.

"May the gentlemen of London be on their guard," he said, "for with both Colette and you, Mother, in the way of assisting Stacey, there will be none who can claim safety." He drank deeply of the wine and again took his seat.

All during the dinner Stacey could feel the glance of the duchess upon her. The conversation at the table was controlled by the DuBois woman and consisted mostly of her recalling bygone times shared by Nigel and herself.

It brought a certain amount of relief to Stacey when the duke excused himself and left the table arm in arm with the Frenchwoman. She herself stood and would have left had not the duchess signaled her to again seat herself.

"Something is amiss, m'lady?" she asked.

The older woman studied her silently for several long moments before saying, "It strikes me that I might have misjudged your innocence, Anastasia."

"I . . . I do not fathom your meaning, m'lady," Stacey answered truthfully.

After a long perusal of her person, the duchess smiled, then chuckled. "Ah, then it was innocence which brought color to your features when Nigel bent over your hand. Excellent. I judged it to be the practiced action of experience."

Color again flooded over Stacey. "Innocence, perhaps, m'lady," she said.

A questioning expression took the duchess. "Aha!" she exclaimed. "Tell me, girl. What was it?"

The color was still high in the girl's face. Her eyes dropped from the direct glance of the duchess. "It was a question from your son, your grace. He would have his jest with me."

Suddenly the duchess laughed. "He again asked of your underclothes, did he?" she got out amid her laughter.

Stacey's eyes met hers instantly. "How did you know of such a thing? He promised . . ."

The duchess waved a hand at her. "No, child, he did not break his promise to you. Your abigail and I had a long talk. So, he observed you in the bath, did he? And even yet, ungentlemanly as it seems, he chooses to tease you of the occurrence and an earlier one."

Stacey's skin flamed with the heat of embarrassment. "He is as an older brother, m'lady," she got out. "He, himself, has said that he is a protector to me. It is only . . ."

The duchess nodded as if in answer to unspoken thoughts. "I know what it is, lass. Well, time enough for that at a later date. Know that I am grateful for your effect on him. To see him smile without bitterness is worth much to me. Now, you must be feeling the strains of the day. It would serve you well to take yourself to your chambers for a night's rest. The morrow will be equally as tiring as your travels have been." She stood, and with a nod, added, "I, too, feel the need of rest. Let us retire."

The words acted as a trigger to Stacey. She got to her feet, a feeling of exhaustion taking her. "I do tire, m'lady. This day has been the most eventful of my entire life. I shall never forget it or your kindness to me. I wish there were a manner in which I could repay your kindness."

The duchess laughed at the statement. "Child,

it is in my thoughts that you will, indeed, repay any kindness done you by me. I foresee that which at this moment is beyond your thinking. If I am correct in my suspicions, and I believe I am, the near future will see to the repaying of all. Now, take yourself to bed. I shall see you in the morning."

Stacey puzzled over the woman's words as she made her way up the stairs to her chambers. Her thoughts were still on the enigma when she slid between the covers to rest. She found sleep would not come instantly as she had imagined it would, Then her thoughts turned to the Frenchwoman and an irritation she would have been unable to explain flowed through her senses. "She seeks Nigel only for her own gain," she said aloud in angry tones. "He is a fool for not realizing it."

Her thoughts were on the man when sleep overtook her.

CHAPTER NINE

Stacey was awakened by Cora moving about the bedroom. Sunlight streamed through the windows to lay a pattern of light and shadows over the bed and her body. "Ah, Cora," she said, sitting up and stretching to the limits of her young muscles. "Such a bed as this makes rest a simple thing. I feel as if I have been reborn overnight."

The abigail smiled at her, saying, "And for the hours you have spent abed, the rebirth could certainly have happened. It is now midmorning. The duchess would not allow me to wake you earlier."

Memory of the planned shopping trip brought the girl from the bed in haste. "Oh, it was planned that we should get an early start for the shops. What must she think of me?"

"She thinks much of you, lass. She has sent messengers to arrange private showings beginning within the hour. Come. Let us see to your toilette.

119

I have spoken to the duchess. There is much I must do, so I will forgo this first visit to the shops. You must hurry."

Stacey descended the stairs into a welter of workmen and decorators all working at top speed to decorate the town house. The duchess stood with two men, giving directions as to the placement of colored ribbons. She noted Stacey suddenly and, with a final word to the workmen, came to meet her.

"Ah, Anastasia. And did you sleep well?"

"Very well, m'lady. I fear I have caused us to be late for our appointed shopping, though."

"Nonsense," the duchess said. "The shopkeepers will wait. For now, you must eat something. Then we shall be on our way. There is much to do between now and tomorrow."

Sending a glance around the busy workmen, Stacey asked, "What is afoot, m'lady?"

"Why, child, there is to be a ball here tomorrow evening. When planned, I had no notion of one such as you being present. It is fortunate as a means to introduce you to London society and give the swains an opportunity to see for what they contend."

A blush took Stacey. "You do too much, m'lady. It is not necessary."

The duchess chuckled. "Well said, girl. But allow an old lady the privilege of enjoying herself as she has not done for years. Come, you must eat." She led the girl to the dining room and called for breakfast.

Stacey had barely begun eating when Nigel stepped into the room to say, "Well, Mother, I am off. I doubt that I shall return before a fortnight." His glance swung to Stacey, and he smiled. "I doubt that I will be missed in the hasty rush of your shopping."

"A fortnight?" the duchess asked. "Impossible. Tomorrow evening is the ball here at Essler House. You would be sorely amiss if you were not present."

A pained expression crossed the duke's face. "Ah, Mother, my feelings for many of those who attend such things are any but pleasant. There is little I would not do to avoid such a thing if I could."

"There is no way for you to avoid it," his mother told him. "Stacey will have her first taste of London society. It is most important to her."

He shrugged in defeat, his sparkling eyes on the girl. "Ah, well, there seems to be no help for it. Very well. I shall return in good time for the gathering. At this rate there will be few of my duties I will have opportunity to see to."

Stacey sensed that his objections were another manner of his teasing her. She smiled slightly, saying, "And is it from the ranks of those you dislike that I am to choose a suitor, brother mine?"

"Hah!" he exclaimed. "There are few enough men in London worthy of my sister's hand. I shall be hard put to find a suitable match for you." He stroked his chin as if in deep concentration. "I believe Lord Rush would be suitable."

"Lord Rush?" Stacey asked, half afraid that he was serious. "And is Lord Rush of quality?"

"And in his seventy-third year," the duchess said, her eyes on the two young people. "A choice I should have expected from you, Nigel. Go on with you. See to what duties you can before the party tomorrow. But be certain you return in time for the first dance with Anastasia."

"I must dance with her?" he demanded in mock disgust. "I'll wager little sister lays claim to a total of two left feet, judging from her country background."

Before Stacey could answer the jibe, the duchess crossed to face the duke, saying, "Enough. Your constant harassment of the girl wears on my nerves. We must concentrate on the preparations. Take yourself to the holdings and allow the shareholders the refreshment of your wit."

Laughing, he turned to leave. At that moment Colette DuBois stepped into the room, pulling soft blue gloves onto her hands. Sending a glance around the three people, she approached Nigel, saying, "You are dressed to travel, Nigel darling. Are you taking yourself from me so soon after my arrival?"

A spot of color appeared above his neckcloth. He sent a glance at Stacey, then said, "My apologies, Colette. It is as I warned you. The duties of the dukedom are many. I must be off to see to them."

"Then I shall ride with you, chéri. It will be a wonderful outing for both of us."

122

The duchess cleared her throat. "It would be impossible. Nigel will be gone overnight. And Anastasia and I are depending upon your expert taste in the choosing of her gown for the party."

Though a pang of misery had invaded Stacey's heart at the thought of the Frenchwoman and Nigel traveling the countryside together, she found the duchess's insistence that the woman be a part of the shopping just as bad. She was torn between a desire to be free of the beautiful woman's company and a fear of what would ensue should Nigel be in constant company with her.

Madame DuBois met the unbending glance of the duchess for a moment as if she would refuse the request. Then, with a shrug, she said to Nigel, "The duchess is correct, of course. There is much I can assist with. Go, chéri. I shall await your return."

The color remained at Nigel's throat and climbed slowly at the words of endearment. Clearing his throat, he bowed slightly to the three women and prepared to take his leave. As he was about to step from the room, he turned long enough to fix Stacey with his eye and say, "Though duty calls for me to share the first dance with you, small sister, you would do well to allow yourself several spots on your card for resting. Feel free to list your older brother in those spots if you wish. There can be none who will argue with such an arrangement." With that he again bowed in her direction and left.

Stacey's heart skipped several beats at his

words. She turned to the older two women and discovered a half smile on the face of the duchess. The Frenchwoman stood staring at her with cold eyes narrowed into slits. The expression of hatred on that face sent a chill of fear through the marrow of the girl. She shuddered involuntarily and got to her feet, unable to speak.

Suddenly, at her movement, the DuBois woman relaxed, and her face fell into a smile. "Older brothers can be such bores," she said. "As if you will tire of the many young men who wish to partake of your time and dances."

Stacey glanced at the duchess and noted a look of expectation on the woman's face. Returning her attention to the Frenchwoman, she returned the smile, saying, "Though older brothers are, at times, boorish, I suspect their intentions are meant for the best interests of younger sisters. I believe I shall do as Nigel suggested. I shall find several resting spots on my dance card for his name."

Color flowed into the older woman's face in spite of the makeup she wore. She would have spoken had it not been for the duchess saying, "Your dance card is your affair, Anastasia. Your wardrobe, however, is mine. Come, child. Make haste with your eating. We must be off to the shops if Madame DuBois and I are to see you properly garbed for the ball."

Stacey thought she detected a note of satisfaction in the statement. She turned back to the breakfast and hurriedly finished.

*　　*　　*

The ride to the trade center of London was made in near silence by the three women. Not once did Madame DuBois speak directly to Stacey. For her portion Stacey was so taken by the sights of the city that she was not aware of the several glances shunted toward her by the Frenchwoman. She was likewise totally unaware of the smile of satisfaction which took that French face only moments before the carriage drew to a stop at the dressmaker's shop.

"Come, Anastasia," the duchess said, getting herself from the carriage. "Though the choice will be small, it will be necessary that for tomorrow's ball, you choose from the gowns already prepared. The others may be of materials of your choice."

Never having owned a true gown in her life, Stacey could only nod. Finally, as she stepped to the walk, she said, "M'lady, I am certain any you select will be appropriate. I fear you have a dunce for a student. I know nothing of what materials gowns are constructed of."

The duchess laughed and sent a glance in the direction of the Frenchwoman. "Ah, madame," she said, "it seems we have our work prepared for us in advance. Let us see to the finest of the ready-made gowns for Anastasia's ball tomorrow."

"Of course," Colette answered with a small smile riding her lips. "We must prepare her in a manner that will draw every eye to her. Something different if possible. Something that no other will be wearing."

The older woman's eyes narrowed at the obvious pleasure in the other's tone. She sent a warning glance at Stacey and entered the shop.

Stacey was amazed at the greeting afforded the duchess, Madame DuBois, and herself. A woman of about forty years glided swiftly across the room to curtsy slightly and say, "Ah, Duchess, it has been such a long period since you have graced this shop with your presence. What is it we can do for you?"

Turning to indicate Stacey, the duchess said, "The girl is in need of a gown for a ball I am giving tomorrow at Essler House. It must be of a cut to call attention to her but not of a garish nature."

"Of course," the woman answered, her expression troubled. "There is the problem of time, your grace. There are very few hours available in this day and tomorrow. It will present many problems as to proper fittings and . . ."

"No bother," the duchess cut her off. "For this occasion Anastasia will choose from the assortment of gowns available in your prepared garments. The others will, of course, be chosen from the material available."

Relief was obvious on the dressmaker's face. Turning, she said, "Come, ladies. Allow me to present those gowns readily available." She led them to chairs and called for several girls to prepare for the showing of gowns. Tea was ordered, and the three women sat waiting for the showing.

The excitement of the moment had Stacey in its firm grip. Her eyes roved over the rich trappings of the shop and the different articles of milady's wardrobe displayed at every wall. She turned to find the amused glance of the duchess on her. Smiling shyly, she said, "I do seem as a child, I know, m'lady. It is only that I have never seen such garments in such abundant numbers."

The duchess chuckled. "Enjoy yourself, girl, for the shops will soon become as everyday things to you. Enjoy them to their fullest while they are still new in your eyes." The dressmaker returned at that moment to announce the beginning of the showing.

A total of twenty-two gowns were presented for their consideration within the next eighty minutes. Stacey sat with wide eyes as each creation was paraded before her. Finally, when the last of the dresses had been shown, she turned to the duchess to say, "It is wonderful, m'lady. Never have I imagined such lovely materials."

The duchess wore a smile. "They are but the smallest sample of what is available, Anastasia. Was there one you found especially attractive?"

"Oh, m'lady, my mind is in such a dither, I could not choose. Pray make the decision for me."

The duchess turned to the Frenchwoman. "And what are your thoughts on the matter, Colette?"

Madame DuBois shrugged, saying, "They are all little better than peasant dresses. However, the yellow silk would seem to be the only suitable one of the lot for Anastasia."

The duchess sat thoughtfully for a long moment before calling for the yellow silk to be reshown. "I thought it to be rather too much if my recollection is correct. It was . . ."

The dressmaker accompanied the model. Approaching the duchess, the woman asked, "Is the gala to be a masquerade, your grace?"

"Of course not," the noblewoman answered.

"Then, I do not understand. The gown's style is not of this time."

Turning to Madame DuBois, the duchess said, "It is of another age, madame. It hardly seems proper for the occasion."

Stacey agreed in her own thoughts. The yellow gown was the one of them all that seemed of a style for the ancient and bitter. Only the model's hands and head were visible outside of the cover of the garment.

"Ah, no, duchess," Madame DuBois said. "It is the very severity of the garment's style which will set Anastasia off from all the rest. Every eye will rest on her, for none will think to wear a matching style."

The duchess studied the gown for a moment before nodding thoughtfully. "Yes, you are correct. I believe you have hit upon it." Without asking Stacey's opinion, she turned to the dressmaker. "The yellow one, there. It will suffice quite well. Take your measurements of the girl and make the necessary alterations. The dress must arrive at Essler House no later than midafternoon tomorrow."

The shopkeeper's reluctant glance went from the gown to Stacey then to the duchess. "Very well, your grace." She turned to Stacey, saying,

"Come, m'lady. It will be necessary to take only a few measurements."

"No," the duchess said. "Allow yourself enough information for the making of several more gowns for which we shall choose the materials. Also, she is in need of all things a young lady should have in the way of undergarments."

With a nod the woman led Stacey behind a curtained alcove and began the measuring process. When the woman was nearly finished, Stacey asked, "You do not fancy the yellow gown the ladies have chosen?"

The shopkeeper met her eyes, attempted a smile, and shrugged. "Let us only say, it would not have been my choice, m'lady. I do, however, have little knowledge of the circumstances where the gown will be worn. The duchess has exquisite taste. I'm sure the choice was a fine one."

Stacey nodded, wishing she'd spoken out against the gown. The thought crossed her mind that Madame DuBois had chosen the gown not because it would enhance her appearance, but for very opposite reasons. Her thoughts shifted to the duchess, and it occurred to her that it was unlikely she would allow her to be improperly dressed for such an event as the ball. A sense of partial reassurance came over her as the seamstress finished her measuring and led her from the alcove.

"Ah, Anastasia," the duchess said as she stepped into view. "Come here, girl. Madame DuBois and I have chosen several of the garments

129

you will need. Now, let us see the materials available for other gowns."

Some time later they left the shop and stepped into the carriage. As Madame DuBois seated herself, the duchess sighed, "I do become forgetful in my dotage. Pardon me, ladies, I must return to the shop and speak of payment for the purchases. I will only be a moment." She stepped back to the walk and entered the shop. Minutes later she was back, the corners of her mouth pulled into a smile. "Now, let us to Essler House. Tea will be waiting. The purchases will be delivered as soon as all is ready with the gown."

CHAPTER TEN

Cora was busily shaking wrinkles from the remaining dresses Stacey had brought from the farm when the girl entered the room to change from her shopping clothes. Leaving the clothing, she asked, "And, Stacey lass, how was your first taste of London shopping?"

"Marvelous, Cora," she answered, "though the gown chosen for the party tomorrow would not have been my selection."

The expression on the girl's face as the words were uttered made the older woman ask, "Is there something amiss with the chosen gown?"

Stacey shrugged. "I know not for sure. The duchess did approve it when the Frenchwoman selected it. It is only that it does hide all of me but my hands and head and appears uncomfortable beyond compare. There is nothing about it to create desire in anyone, if what I've heard of men is true."

Cora chuckled shortly. "Concern yourself not, lass. If the duchess agreed with the selection, there is little to worry about. She would not lead you astray."

The girl nodded. "I only hope you are right, Cora. Though all the other gowns shown us were of dimensions to expose a portion of a woman's arms and . . ." She colored slightly and averted her eyes.

". . . bosom? Is that the word you searched for?"

Stacey nodded. "Though it does seem outrageous of me, I would at least allow him to know that I possess skin below my neck."

"Him?" Cora asked. "Is it the duke you speak of?"

Again Stacey colored. "I meant them—the men who will attend the party."

"Of course. Well, change into something more relaxing. The duchess and the French one will surely expect your company for lunch."

"And for tea," Stacey said, suddenly moving to change. "Time does slip away from me. Tea is being served at this moment."

After assisting her in the change, Cora watched with a smile as the girl hurried from the room. "Ah, lass," she said when Stacey had gone, "a pity you must grow up in so short a time."

The duchess sat with a cup of tea in hand when Stacey entered the room. Hesitating, the girl sent a glance around the room in search of Madame DuBois.

"If it is the Frenchwoman you seek, Anastasia, she is not feeling well. It seems the strain of choosing your gown for the party was too much for her. She is lying down in her quarters. Come, sit beside me and tell me your opinions of London from what you have noted thus far."

Relieved that the DuBois woman was not present, Stacey accepted tea from the servant and took a seat beside the duchess. "There are many things which amaze me about the city, your grace," she said when she was comfortable. "It is as if an entirely new world has opened before me. I feel there is such an abundance of the new, I shall never be able to see it all."

The older woman nodded. "So it seems to all on their first visit to London, lass. You will, however, find that the sights, as well as the shops, will become commonplace to you before many weeks have passed." She hesitated a moment, then said, "I understand from Nigel that you exacted a promise from him to the effect that you could return to your farm upon your marriage. Is it still your wish to do so?"

Stacey was surprised to find that she had not thought of her former home nor her father in some time. She took a moment to consider her feelings in silence. Then, her eyes meeting those of the duchess squarely, she shook her head. "The farm and the life I led there do seem far in the past, your grace. I wonder that such a thing can be, but it is so. Would that I could be fortunate enough to spend the rest of my days as this one has been spent thus far."

A smile of understanding crossed the face of the duchess. "Concern yourself not, child. There is no reason for you to leave Essler House until it is of your own choosing. Now, tell me, what is your opinion of the gown and trappings chosen for you by Madame DuBois and myself?"

It was in the girl to state her misgivings at the choice of gowns. But fear of offending the duchess made her say, "Your choice can only be for my best benefit, your grace. I feel you are much superior to myself in such matters."

"And Madame DuBois? Do you now believe her to be in your favor, also?"

Their eyes met. Stacey hesitated only a moment before saying, "No, your grace. I believe that one to be as we discussed earlier. I feel she wishes me to appear as a fool before the world if at all possible."

"And you think I would allow such a thing to happen?"

"Oh no, your grace. Only moments ago Cora and I discussed the fact that you would do nothing ill for me. I know the choice of gown was the best or you would have made remark."

"Good. The gown will call attention to you, rest assured. It will open the eyes of all who attend the party. Do not concern yourself about it. Now, is there anything you would do with the remaining portion of the day?"

"I would, if possible, take further tour of London, m'lady. It is, as I have said, the opening of a new world to me. I would fill my eyes with the sights."

The duchess nodded. "Very well, then. When we have lunched, we shall summon the carriage and the two of us and your Cora shall view that which is to be seen in London. I fear you will find many things disappointing within the boundaries of the city. There are many returned from the wars who have little to do in the manner of work. The city is full of those who must steal or starve. Nigel has fought for passage of monies to ease the plight of these former soldiers but to no avail. Ah well, perhaps one day . . ."

"Your son does appear to be of a sensitive nature where his fellow man is concerned," the girl answered. "Would that all men were of such feelings."

"You are correct. Nigel cares deeply for all who are needy. Well, enough of this. Come, let us lunch and be gone. There is much to see. I shall enjoy being a guide to you and Cora for the afternoon."

Dusk was upon the city when the carriage again drew to a stop at Essler House. Both Stacey and Cora felt the exhaustion of their visit in the city. Only the duchess seemed as fresh as the moment they had left Essler House.

"You do amaze me, your grace," Cora said as they entered the house. "I feel as if I have walked the entire distance to Brensloe and back."

"Age teaches one to pace oneself," the duchess answered with a smile. "However, I doubt that I should last an hour if I were to match myself with you on the farm. It is all in what a person becomes used to."

Stacey chucked lightly. "Considering the energy you have shown this day, m'lady, I doubt that the farm would slow you at all. I feel the need of bath and rest."

Upon entering the house, the duchess called for hot water to be taken to the women's rooms and gave the cook directions for the evening meal. In all corners of the house decorations and preparations were obvious reminders of the party planned for the next day. Stacey turned to Cora as they mounted the stairs toward their rooms.

"The thought of tomorrow's festivities brings a tenseness to my muscles, Cora," she said. "I pray my reactions to all will be within the bounds of propriety. I would not embarrass the duchess or the duke."

"Rest your concern, child," the abigail told her. "You will do fine. There will be but a few moments at first when your nerves will stretch thin. Then you will find yourself falling into the swim of things. Come now, to your bath. Would you have me assist you with your clothing?"

"It is not necessary, Cora," the girl answered with a yawn. "I will be taxed to remain awake once the warm water surrounds me."

"See that your door is bolted before you step into the tub, lass. It would not do to have a reoccurrence of the earlier mishap."

Color rose in the girl's face at the statement. Without answering, she entered her room, her

136

thoughts on the occasion only days before when the duke had entered the room at the inn and observed her in the bath. Crossing to the bed, she settled herself to await the arrival of the bath water. A smile played across her face as she recalled the last words uttered by Cora outside her doorway. "Is it possible," she asked herself aloud, "that I do, indeed, set my cap for the duke without realizing it?" She was still considering her feelings along that line when the tap came at the door and two servants brought the steaming water into the room. When they had gone, she crossed to bolt the door and then removed her clothing. She was about to step into the tub when she caught sight of herself in the mirror of the far wall. She hesitated, guiltily, then stepped to the glass and surveyed herself.

Sliding her hands over her boyish hips, she knew a moment of frustration. She turned to allow a side view of herself and said, "Ah well, Stacey, there is little there for any such as the duke to be attracted by. Would that you had the bosom of the Frenchwoman to catch the eye of such as he." Her good mood evaporating, she crossed to the tub and submerged herself in the heady warmth of the water. She scrubbed herself with a vengeance, making short work of the bath.

The anger dissipated as she toweled herself dry. Though her mood was far from what it had been earlier, she again stepped to position before the mirror, thinking, Even so, it was his statement that the birthmark and all it protected was attractive. She frowned suddenly, then met her own eyes in the reflection from the mirror. "You are past the age of self-deceit, Stacey Griffith," she told the reflection. "It is to be admitted that you desire more than brotherly love from the duke." Her eyes filled suddenly with the admission, and she crossed to the bed to throw herself facedown, her shoulders suddenly racked with the effort of uncontrolled tears. "And his eyes are only for the Frenchwoman," she sobbed into the coverlet.

Some time later the harsh sounds of rapping on the door awoke her. She lay for a long moment in confusion, then Cora's call snapped her to her senses. Pushing herself from the bed, she was about to tell the woman to enter when she realized that she was without clothes.

"One moment, Cora," she called, hurriedly moving to wrap a robe around herself. When the garment was in place, she crossed to unbolt the door and swing it open.

"Why, lass," Cora exclaimed as she stepped across the threshold, "you are not yet dressed. Dinner has been announced. Hurry, you must don your gown and join the duchess."

"Ah, Cora, it appears I did fall asleep after my bath. It will take but a moment for me to slip into the clothing and join the duchess." She turned to the huge wardrobe and in so doing stepped in front of the mirror. Her reflection from the glass recalled the admission she had wrung from herself earlier. She faltered, a hand going to her forehead. "Oh, Cora, I know not what to do with myself."

"What is it, child?" the abigail asked, moving to

place a hand on the girl's arm. "What is amiss with you?"

Stacey turned to face her, tears again threatening to overflow her eyelids. "I feel I have acted the fool with my emotions, Cora," she said. "I have discovered something about myself which can lead to nothing but eternal heartbreak for me. Oh, what am I to do?"

Cora studied her for a long moment before nodding. A smile began at the corners of her mouth and spread to capture her face. "Ah, Stacey," she cooed, "you have realized where your heart lies, have you?"

The girl's head came up. Her eyes widened slightly. "What? You knew? But . . ."

Cora nodded in satisfaction. "You are simple to read, girl. The moment the duke comes near, you become as lighted as the lamps of London in the dark of night. There was little doubt in my mind from the first." She paused, the smile vanishing from her face. "But you cause yourself undue stress, lass. The duke is not for such as you. Release yourself from such cravings and consider those who will be acquainting themselves with you tomorrow evening."

Stacey, her eyes filled to overflowing, nodded. "It is as I have said, Cora. It can lead to nothing but heartbreak for me. I would have no other than Nigel. The thought of another's touch sickens me. Oh, what am I to do?"

Cora considered the plight of the girl for a long moment before saying, "It would serve you well to speak of this to the duchess, lass. It is my feeling that she, of all available, would advise you best. Now dry your eyes and don your clothing. Dinner awaits and the duchess must surely grow curious at your absence."

Removing the robe, Stacey allowed the abigail to assist her with the dressing. Then, as she was about to leave the room, she turned to ask, "You truly believe the duchess will understand my meaning should I ask for her advice, Cora?"

"As no other could, lass. Believe me, the woman loves you as a daughter. Confide in her. She will understand and know what to tell you."

The duchess and the Frenchwoman were at the table when Stacey made her way into the dining room and took her seat.

"We had begun to think you were ill, girl," the duchess said, an expression of curiosity in her face. "Was the view of London's sights too much for you?"

Stacey met the old eyes and shook her head. "No, m'lady. I napped after the bath. I'm sorry I was late." She forced herself to look to the Frenchwoman. "And are you feeling better, madame?"

The DuBois woman nodded. "Much, child. I fear I am not accustomed to the air of London. The visit to the shops this morning had its way with me. I, too, required a nap to return me to my normal self."

"You seem nervous, child," the duchess said. "Are you sure you are not ailing?"

"I am fine, m'lady," Stacey answered. "I would

have a moment of your time following the meal if I may."

"Certainly," the duchess said, her eyes narrowing slightly as she studied the girl's face. After a moment of perusal, she chuckled, "It would be a blow to London if you should not be of fine health to attend the party tomorrow evening. I look forward to the expressions on the faces of all those who tout their daughters as the toast of this season."

Color swept into Stacey's face at the compliment. "Thank you, m'lady. I only hope I do not disappoint you."

"And you shall not," the duchess laughed. "Concern yourself not on that score, girl. You shall do fine. Now, let us eat. Then we shall take our leave from Madame DuBois for a moment and see to your problem, whatever it might be."

CHAPTER ELEVEN

Stacey was relieved when the dinner was completed and she and the duchess made their way from the presence of the Frenchwoman. When they had entered the study and closed the door, the duchess turned to her to ask, "Well, Anastasia, what is it? During dinner you seemed strung taut. Are you so concerned about the party?"

Stacey shook her head and dropped her glance. "No, m'lady, only in the respect that it is to be of no avail. I feel I have used you ill without intention."

The older woman crossed to her, saying, "Look at me, child. You have nothing to fear from me or any in this house. Explain your words and your concern."

Steeling herself, Stacey met the woman's glance. "The party makes it possible for me to be introduced to the young gentlemen of London, does it not?"

"In a manner of speaking, yes."

"Then, m'lady, you expend your energies in my direction for nothing, I fear. The party will be little but a dismal failure."

For a long moment the duchess stood silently. Then, with a wave of her hand toward a small couch, she said, "All right, Anastasia, sit down and tell me what concerns you so. The party is not the nub of the matter, I'm sure. Now, tell me. What is it?"

Seating herself, Stacey put her attention on her clasped hands and said, "I fear there is little use of my meeting any of the young men of the city, m'lady. It would be to no avail. There will be none I could care for."

Again the duchess was silent. Finally the beginning of a smile tugging at her lips, she said, "And that, too, must be explained, Anastasia. Why is it you feel so about the young swains you have not yet met?"

The girl twisted her hands in anguish for a long moment before saying, "I am entranced with another. Though he knows nor cares not of it, m'lady, there is no other I would have in this life." The words came out in a rush, and she lifted her eyes to meet those of the duchess. "The party will do nothing but sadden you, m'lady."

The duchess chuckled, a broad smile on her face. "Sadden me, child? You are wrong. It will be the making of me, now that I am aware of my duties where you are concerned."

144

"But it can serve no useful purpose, m'lady. It can only disappoint you in your plans for my season. You do not understand what I am . . ."

"I understand perfectly, Anastasia," the duchess said kindly. "Do you believe me blind?"

Confusion registered itself on the girl's face. "M'lady?" she asked.

The chuckle came again as the duchess got to her feet to cross to the window and stare out across the Essler property. After a moment of such viewing, she turned back to fix Stacey with a sympathetic glance. "Ah, Anastasia, to be able to share your innocence and youth at this moment is of great value to me. You, alone, of the women in this house were unaware of your feelings for Nigel. And now that you have realized the truth, you feel I waste my efforts to make you the toast of London."

Stacey's mouth dropped open at the words. She stuttered for a moment before getting out, "You knew, m'lady? How could you? I . . ."

"You are, as I said earlier, as an open book. Your love for my son is obvious the moment he comes into your view. If you will recall, I mentioned that the Frenchwoman recognized the truth the moment she met you."

Stacey colored slightly and dropped her glance. "I would not have had such a thing happen for all the wealth in London, m'lady. I meant no malice toward you." She lifted her glance and wiped at the tears which formed in her eyes. "I was not aware of such a thing happening to me, m'lady."

"And why do the tears come, child? Such a realization is cause for joy, not sadness. Is there some problem I do not know about?"

"Only that it can never be, m'lady. I realize that. Do not fear, I shall not embarrass you where Nigel is concerned. I will endeavor to remain out of his company as much as possible."

"Nonsense," the duchess snapped. "How can you possibly hope to win him if you are forever making yourself scarce from him. Can you not see the possibilities of the party tomorrow? Do you believe Nigel will be unaware of the glances and attention you will receive from the young men who are present? Unless I misguess, he will find himself as taken up with his feelings as you are with yours at this moment. I would judge he will make use of every space allowed him on your program."

Stacey found it impossible to believe what she had heard. "M'lady, do you suggest that you wish your son to love me as I love him? I thought . . ."

"That I wish? What I wish would have little bearing on the matter, Anastasia. For, though he realizes it not, he already loves you. It requires only a method to make him aware of his feelings, and tomorrow's party could well afford us that method."

"And you sympathize with me in this, m'lady? I cannot believe you would . . ."

"And what is so preposterous about such a thing, girl? Why is it you believe yourself unworthy of my son?"

Her senses swimming, Stacey sat without speaking for several seconds. Then, her tone apologetic, she said, "M'lady, I am truly confused. Nigel is all

I wish for in this life. That would mean, if it were possible for him to feel in the same manner toward me, that I would become . . ."

"The young Duchess of Essler," the duchess finished for her. "That, unfortunately, is one of the requirements when you wed a duke, Anastasia. It can be no other way, I fear."

"You would allow me to become the duchess, m'lady?"

"I shall help you in any way possible, child. You are, though young, of good carriage and quick mind. The duties of your position require such." She studied the girl for a moment before adding, "Yes, you will make a lovely duchess."

Suddenly Stacey was on her feet, moving toward the older woman. "Oh, m'lady," she sighed as the duchess took her to her bosom, "not in my wildest dreams that I imagined such a thing could be. I feared so that you would crush me when you knew."

Pushing the girl back to arm's length, the duchess said, "And crush you I will if you are not at your most fetching tomorrow for the party. If we are to bring Nigel to his senses, we must use all the weapons at our disposal."

"The Frenchwoman will . . ."

"She will spend her every moment attempting to turn Nigel's feelings toward her," the duchess said. "It will require that you be alert at all times lest she make you appear the fool."

"But Nigel is taken with her. He held her in his arms and kissed her when she appeared at this house. They are as lovers."

147

"Bah! Nigel is as ignorant of his true feelings as you were of your own. There is no love in his heart for the woman. But until he is made to realize where his true feelings lie, there is a danger that she will see to the success of her endeavors and convince him to marry her. Men are fools for the most part where affairs of the heart are concerned. It will be up to us to make certain that such a thing does not take place."

Stacey turned from her with a distressed sigh. "Ah, m'lady, she is so beautiful. How can Nigel possibly see me when such a one is there to take his every glance and fill his eye with such loveliness?"

"Her edges, unlike yours, are rough, Anastasia. There will come a time when that will become plain to Nigel. It is only for us to see that the time comes before he commits himself to marriage with her. Now, we must return to her company. Control yourself, girl. Tomorrow will see to the beginning of our campaign. I feel you will surprise all, including yourself, when you make entrance to the party. Come, let us rejoin our guest." Taking the girl by the arm, she led the way from the study. "Control your feelings, Anastasia," she warned as they entered the parlor.

"I shall try, m'lady," Stacey answered.

Madame DuBois sat waiting for them when they entered the parlor. She smiled at the duchess and asked, "And do you or Anastasia play the spinet, m'lady?"

The duchess sent a questioning glance at Stacey. "Are you adept at the keyboard, Anastasia?"

"No, m'lady," Stacey answered. "There was little time and never enough money for such things on the farm."

The duchess turned back to the Frenchwoman. "In my younger days I played a bit. It has, however, been many years since I've sat at the instrument. Do you play, madame?"

Madame DuBois nodded. "A fortunate accomplishment of mine. Many were the times during the sadness and tragedy of war that I played for Nigel. It was, I believe, what kept his sanity ofttimes." Her glance was on Stacey as she made the statement.

"It would perhaps pass the evening the quicker if you would play something for us, madame," the duchess said, aware of the irritation building in the young girl.

"It would be my pleasure to play for you, Duchess," Madame DuBois said, rising to cross to the spinet. It took only a few moments for both the duchess and Stacey to realize that the woman was indeed an accomplished musician. The notes trickled from the instrument as water over the stones in a singing brook. When she had completed the first song, she turned to smile at them. "It has been so long I fear my fingers have stiffened."

"It was remarkable," the duchess told her and turned to Stacey. "Don't you think so, Anastasia?"

Stacey nodded. "It was very nice, madame. You are truly fine at the keyboard."

"Do play more, madame," the duchess said, an

149

amused smile playing at the edges of her lips. "The sounds make the evening more pleasant."

Smiling, the woman again turned to the keyboard and played. Some thirty minutes later she struck a final chord and stood, saying, "Ah, there is little in this world as fulfilling as music. Too long at it tires one, though. If I may take my leave, Duchess, I would retire for the night. I feel the party tomorrow will call for all our energies if we are to present the child as she should be presented."

The duchess nodded. "You are correct, madame. We should all take to our beds and gain the rest available. Tomorrow will, indeed, be a strenuous day for all of us." So saying, she stood and with a glance at Stacey, said, "Come, Anastasia. Though you are not aware of it, Madame DuBois has the right of it. Your first party in London will be tiring to the extreme. You should get all the rest you can."

"Yes, m'lady," Stacey said as the Frenchwoman left the room. "I wish for the words to thank you for the pleasure you have brought to my heart this day, m'lady. The feeling of being in a dream is still upon me. I only wish never to awaken."

. The duchess laughed at the statement. "Ah, Anastasia, some day you will know the trials of motherhood and the concern of a mother that her child not make a mistake. You judge yourself too harshly and concern yourself too much with the social stations you imagine yourself outside of. Come, child, to your bed and rest. Tomorrow will see the return of Nigel. It would not do for him see you in haggard condition."

The words had the desired effect on the girl. She raised a hand to her cheek as if in search of telltale wrinkles and said, "I would have Nigel see me as the desire of his life, m'lady. I shall take myself to bed as you recommend. May your night pass as pleasantly as the last hours have for me, your grace." Together the women left the parlor.

Her heart was aflutter when she traversed the stairs and entered the bedroom. She laughed in happiness as she closed the door behind her and leaned back against it.

"And what has taken you in such manner, child," the waiting Cora asked, laying aside her needlepoint. "Has the evening gone to your liking?"

"Oh, Cora," Stacey exclaimed happily, "you will not believe what has occurred. The duchess wishes me for the wife of Nigel. She told me so. She . . ."

"Here, here, Stacey," the abigail said, smiling at the happiness displayed by the girl. "You'll strain something if you continue as you are. Did the lady, indeed, indicate her liking for your position and feelings? I would not have supposed it."

"Oh, she did, Cora. She is wonderful. She wishes me to be the young Duchess of Essler. She has said it."

Laughing, Cora approached her, saying, "Then it would seem you have little to concern yourself with, Stacey. Now it is time for you to take yourself beneath the covers and rest. Tomorrow will be more pleasant and more strenuous than this day has been, I'll warrant. Come, out of your clothes and into your nightgown."

Still bubbling, the girl allowed the abigail to assist her and moments later she slid into the bed. "It is wonderful, Cora," she breathed. "I know I shall not be able to sleep the entire night, my heart beats so."

Cora chuckled in understanding. "Put your head to the pillow, girl. Though you feel it impossible, sleep will come. May your dreams be as pleasant as your day has been. I shall see you in the morning. Her grace informed me that a hairdresser will arrive in the afternoon to see to the styling of your hair. There is that and also the wealth of other things which must be seen to before the party begins. Sleep, child." She turned and was almost to the door when Stacey called to her. Turning, she asked, "Yes, Stacey, what is it?"

"I really do love him, Cora. More than anything in the world. Is that wrong?"

Cora shook her head in answer. "No, lass, it is not wrong. And there is no question in me of your feelings toward him. May God see to it that you have your heart's desire and a life of happiness with him."

"Thank you, Cora," she said, again sliding her head to the pillow. "If only the duchess is correct in her thinking of his feelings."

"She is wise beyond the limits of most I have known, Stacey. Trust her judgment. She would know better than any other of her son's feelings. Now put the light out and let sleep come. The world will be here when you awaken." So saying, the abigail stepped from the room, leaving a happy Stacey Griffith behind.

"Ah," Stacey said as she snuffed out the bedside light, "may Nigel make haste in coming back to me. There is much he must find out if he is to make me as his duchess." With the thought still in mind, she lay quietly in the darkness, a smile on her face.

CHAPTER TWELVE

Sunlight streamed through the window and caressed Stacey's cheeks with warmth. She awoke slowly and for a moment lay as she was, reflecting on the strangeness of the dream she had had. It took her several minutes to realize the dream had been reality. Then, as the realization came, she sat up in the bed to exclaim aloud, "She wishes me as daughter-in-law." The next moment her thoughts turned to the return of Nigel, and she leaped from the bed to prepare herself for meeting him. She was at the wardrobe studying on which of her dresses to wear when a light tap came at the door. Crossing to open it a crack, she asked, "Who is it?"

"It is Cora, girl. I wondered if you were about as yet. I'll have water brought up for you."

"Thank you, Cora," she answered. "The day is a beautiful one."

The abigail laughed. "For one of your feelings, it would be such if rain were pouring. I shall return when I have arranged for your bath water."

Stacey was again at the wardrobe when Cora returned to the room. She turned, an expression of anguish on her face, as the abigail entered. "Oh, Cora," she exclaimed, "there is nothing here I would have Nigel see me in on his return to Essler House. Why are all the dresses so plain and unattractive?"

Smiling, the abigail crossed to lift a soft blue dress from the wardrobe. "And but a few days ago this was your favorite of all the dresses in the world, child. How is it that it is now plain and unattractive?"

Stacey sighed. "The Frenchwoman would never wear such a one as that even in her worst moment, Cora. Nigel will consider me as only a farm girl, I fear."

"And, until recently, you will recall, such was the case. Come. The duke has had opportunity to see you as a farm girl. I doubt your knowing of your love for him will alter anything about you in his eyes."

The bath water arrived, and Cora moved to lay out underclothing for the girl. When Stacey returned from the bath, she again spoke of the plainness of the available clothing.

With a sigh Cora said, "Child, there is nothing to be done about it at this moment. In a week, perhaps two, your wardrobe will be complete. Trust what you have. It will do, I assure you."

Reluctantly the girl donned underclothes and

the dress. When she was dressed, she pirouetted before the mirror, saying, "It will be little enough he will see to find pleasure in, Cora. Ah, that I might have but one of the gowns favored by the Frenchwoman."

"Waste not your envy on her, Stacey," Cora advised. "She is as she is and you are as you are. There is nothing of her being which would fit you comfortably, in dress or feeling. Be yourself, girl. Do not attempt to become as another. It can only lead to your appearing foolish."

Realizing the truth in the statement, Stacey nodded. "You are correct, Cora. I am so taken up with my feelings for Nigel, I would do anything to insure he notice me with favor. I must, this moment, cease thinking as a child. I am Anastasis Griffith, not a Madame DuBois from France." Her eyes filmed suddenly and she added in half sob, "Though I would give my all for her knowledge in attracting Nigel."

"Enough, girl," Cora scolded. "You do prattle on as a love-sick child. Comb your hair and take yourself from this room. The duke will arrive and you will see him again. It is only your eyes which will see the situation differently. He will remain as he was when he left. Now, go. You look fine."

With the abigail's words ringing in her ears, she made her way down the stairs and breakfasted alone. She was finishing the meal when the duchess entered the room to say, "The day is a beautiful one, Anastasia. I thought of waking you to show you the grounds of Essler House, but the thought came to me that you might have been troubled with gaining sleep last night. You must, at a later date, join me in my early morning walks about the grounds. I never tired of this place."

Stacey found herself surprised that the woman had been awake and around the grounds at such an hour. "I imagined you still abed, m'lady," she said honestly. "The sun's rays were but newborn when they awoke me."

Laughing, the duchess took a chair across from her. "There are few mornings of the world when I lay abed until the break of dawn, child. There are many bowers and other sites which have their full and finest beauty only when touched by the coming of the new day. One day soon you will discover this. You will find much to love here."

"And does Nigel walk the early morning away, also, m'lady?"

"That one? No. Though there are few mornings I am about before him, he uses the hours to concern himself with the problems of Napoleon. He spends his walking time in the study, more is the pity. It would be well if he could be persuaded to take himself to the gardens for even a few minutes."

Coloring slightly, Stacey said, "M'lady, I would know all possible of Nigel. What is his concern with Napoleon? Why does he drive himself so?"

"Nigel has been convinced since the exile that Napoleon will again attempt to capture and enslave Europe. Though I find it difficult to believe such a thing, I realize that Nigel is above all others in knowledge of the little emperor. But as to his concern, my son is a chief advisor to the War

Council. It is his knowledge of Napoleon which has brought the station about. The duty rests heavily on his shoulders, for none there share his beliefs of Bonaparte's determination. You must realize, child, that until he came upon you, he seldom smiled nor had a moment for thoughts of his own pleasure. For that, I am eternally grateful to you."

"I only wish I could remove all problems from his shoulders, m'lady."

Nodding her satisfaction with the girl's reaction, the duchess said, "And as the young Duchess of Essler, such will be your responsibility. As wife to him, you become helpmate and confidante as well. It will be yours to see that he has an attentive ear to fill with his problems and a willing lover to ease the tensions of his body." She hesitated momentarily, studying the girl. "Did I say something amiss, Anastasia? Your expression has taken on a new meaning."

Shaking her head, Stacey answered happily, "Oh no, m'lady. You have said nothing amiss. It is only that you referred to me as the young Duchess of Essler. The title attached to my person does send a thrill through my body. I still find your faith and acceptance beyond belief. There is much I must learn from you if I am to assume the duties of duchess."

Smiling, the duchess started to speak, hesitated as if listening, then said, "Enough, child. Unless my ears deceive me, our guest is about. Control the happiness which your face makes plain. It would take little for her to fathom the reason for such a feeling. There is no need for us to allow her any advantage to her aims."

The words were no more than spoken when Madame DuBois stepped into the room, saying, "It seems I've overslept, m'lady. I was of the impression that breakfast was at an hour the same as yesterday."

"It is nothing, madame," the duchess assured her. "Breakfast hour is when you wish. Anastasia has only this moment finished."

The Frenchwoman shook her head as if to remove the last trace of deep sleep. "The early morning hours are the worst of the day for one such as myself. I have only moments ago awakened thinking that I was the first of the house awake."

"It is of no concern, madame," the duchess answered. "Anastasia and I were about to prepare for the return of the workmen who decorate for the party. I would have the preparations complete before Nigel returns."

"And when shall we expect my Nigel, m'lady?" the Frenchwoman asked, the words falling from her tongue in a confidence not lost on Stacey.

The duchess hesitated only a moment before saying, "I imagine he will arrive in time for the noon meal. There is much in the way of preparation he must see to before he takes Anastasia to the dance floor for the first dance." She turned to Stacey. "Come, child. The workmen will be arriving soon. Let us decide on the placement of the final decorations. Madame DuBois can join us when she has eaten." With a nod in the French-woman's direction, she led Stacey from the dining room.

Anger was fast taking the girl as she followed the duchess. When they had stepped from earshot of Madame DuBois, she exclaimed, "Oh, I hate her. I hate her for waking in such beauty and I hate her for assuming Nigel is hers. It will not be easy for me to contain my feelings, m'lady."

A bitter chuckle escaped the duchess's lips. "You assume too much to be true, Anastasia. Her statement of being awake only moments was meant to accomplish exactly what it did. She has, with a simple lie, undermined what confidence you had in yourself."

"A lie, m'lady? I don't understand."

"Light was visible at her window for some time during my travels about the grounds, child. The beauty she claims to have awakened with required more than an hour of preparation on her part unless I am mistaken. As to her reference to Nigel, people own things, not other people. She has a ready quiver of arrows at her command, I must admit. But you must take all she says and insinuates in your stride. Otherwise she will appear the better of the two."

"Yes, m'lady. Oh, that I could read her as you do. I feel lost in a sea of confusion ofttimes."

"That will pass, child. Now we must decide on the arrangement of the final decorations. Put your mind to it."

* * *

It was nearing midday when the duchess, her keen glance on every step of the work, suddenly called to a workman who worked from a tall ladder. "No, man," she exclaimed, "it is not draped right. Have you no eyes for symmetry? Oh, that I were of younger years and could mount the ladder myself."

Turning from her work with other decorations, Stacey said, "Might I hang the bunting, m'lady? If you will but advise me from the floor, I'm sure we would make a job of it." She was already moving toward the ladder and signaling the workman to come down as she spoke.

"Very well, Anastasia," the duchess agreed. "See to it that you retain your balance on the ladder, though. It would not do for you to injure yourself."

"There have been many ladders to climb during my years on the farm," the girl answered, making her way up to the top of the ladder and attacking the bunting. She held it against the wall and looked to the duchess for directions.

"Up a bit, girl, slowly. There, right there. That is the place. Mark it and let the workman finish it."

Turning back to the bunting, Stacey marked the spot where the attachment was to be made. She was about to make her way down the ladder when from below her Nigel asked, "And what have we here? Has my little sister become a common workman while I have been absent?"

His voice brought her around on the ladder. Her footing slipped, and she pitched headlong toward the floor. A scream left her lips as the ladder went sideways.

The next moment, as her breath left her completely, her body came to a sudden stop in the arms of Nigel. He stood holding her as a child for several moments, concern obvious in his eye. Then, as she sighed heavily, he smiled and hoisted her up and over his shoulder as he would a sack of grain. "Mother," he called to the alarmed duchess, "take note that Stacey makes all haste when coming from a ladder. It is good to see the young do not waste time with mundane things."

Stacey squirmed in his grip and pummeled his back with her fists. His laughter only increased her attack on his person. "Put me down, put me down," she demanded. "If not for you, I would have been safe as any."

"Enough, Nigel," the duchess said, a smile of relief and understanding on her face. "Put the girl on her feet. Must you always be at her so?"

The duke did as ordered. Still chuckling, he faced a florid Stacey, saying, "Ah, little sister, your anger comes on you as quickly as you come off a ladder. Are you injured?"

"Only my pride," she got out, turning away from him. She stopped in mid-stride as she met the eyes of Madame DuBois, who stood across the great hall giving directions to workmen. The naked hatred in those eyes stopped the girl in her tracks, and she turned to the duchess. "I think I had best lie down a moment, m'lady. The fall did take the nerve from my body."

The duchess, too, had been aware of the expression in the Frenchwoman's face. She nodded to Stacey. "A narrow escape such as that would affect anyone, Anastasia. Go to your room and rest if your older brother will hold his humor in harness long enough to allow you past him."

"Nigel," the Frenchwoman exclaimed as if she'd only then become aware of the duke's presence. "And was your trip rewarding?" Coming swiftly across the room, she placed a kiss on his cheek. "I have missed you, chéri. You must not take yourself from me again for so long a period."

Stacey swept from the room and made her way up the stairs to her quarters. She slammed the door irritably behind her and threw herself on the bed. "I hate her," she growled into the mattress. Then her thoughts turned to the accident and Nigel holding her in his arms. He is strong beyond belief, she told herself. Getting up from the bed, she crossed to the mirror and worked a comb through her hair in an attempt to repair the dishevelment caused by the toil of the day. I shall return to his presence. Madame DuBois will not have him to herself this day. So deciding, she left the room and returned to the great hall.

Only the duchess was in attendance when she entered the hall. She sent a quick glance around and knew a moment of sadness when her eyes did not fall on Nigel. She would have left to return to her room had not the duchess called to her.

"Anastasia," the older woman said, "Nigel has

gone to his room to refresh himself from his travels. Madame DuBois left to walk the grounds with a veiled hint to him that she would be awaiting his company when he desired."

Defeat hit Stacey like a hammer. She allowed her emotions to show in her face, though she fought against such a display in front of the duchess. "I sense the woman is too much for the knowledge I have, m'lady," she got out. "There is nothing I can do to offset her quick mind."

The duchess crossed to her and laid a hand upon her arm. "Come, child, think of what I have just said concerning Madame DuBois. Does nothing avail itself to you in method of gaining Nigel's company for yourself?"

Stacey shook her head in despair. "To accomplish such a thing, I would have to face him at the staircase as he descended and force my attentions on him. No. There is no . . ."

"Exactly," the duchess said. "I was certain you would see the solution once you considered it. Now, go. Within a short time Nigel will leave his room and make his way down the staircase. As you have decided, that would be an excellent time for you to ask him to show you about the grounds of Essler House. Go, child."

"But . . . but she will be waiting, your grace. It will be to no avail, I fear."

Smiling, the duchess turned the girl toward the door, saying, "True, she will be waiting. But for Nigel, not for Nigel and his adopted little sister. Do not be surprised if Madame DuBois chooses to pass up the tour of the grounds when you and Nigel meet with her. Now go, child, lest you miss him."

Stacey arrived at the bottom of the staircase just as Nigel set foot on the top step. Pausing, she sent a glance up at him and marveled that her blood could flow so quickly at the mere sight of the man. Then he noticed her.

Smiling up at him, she said, "And, big brother, since you have near done for me this day, would it be too much to ask to be shown the grounds of this beautiful home?"

His smile matched hers as he made his way down the stairs. "You choose the ideal moment for such a request, spoiled sister of mine. I am on my way to escort Colette on a tour of the same grounds you wish to see. Come, you shall join us. Only be warned, I will apply correction to your backside once again should you trouble me." Taking her arm as he gained the ground floor, he led her toward the rear of the house. As they passed the great hall, the duchess stepped from the door and sent a satisfied glance at them.

"Stacey has decided she should be knowledgeable of the property, Mother," Nigel said, "though I sense with your plans for her, she will spend little enough time here. We will be in the gardens with Madame DuBois should you want us."

"Very well," the duchess told him. "See to it that you do not allow yourself to be gone too long. The guests will be arriving in only a few hours. Anastasia must endure the efforts of the

166

hairdresser an hour before that." She sent a glance at Stacey as she moved past them. Her right eye closed in a wink toward the girl and then she was gone.

CHAPTER THIRTEEN

They came upon the Frenchwoman in a garden seat amidst a wealth of flowers. Her glance came up as Nigel spoke. The alluring smile she wore lasted only until she became aware of Stacey, then her lips thinned for a split second as she rose to meet him.

"Ah, Colette," Nigel said, "we are in luck. Stacey has decided to join us for our tour of the grounds. Come, we shall enjoy the gardens together."

For a moment it seemed the woman would lash out at him. Then the smile again took her face, and she said, "How nice. Tell me, has the great hall been decorated to completion?"

Nigel shrugged. "To my way of thinking, it has. What difference if a piece of color is missing. There will be few there who have eyes for any but Stacey and the others who prepare for the coming

169

season. Come, let us relax a moment before the party is upon us."

"Of course," Madame DuBois agreed—to Stacey's dismay. "Where shall we begin our tour of these lovely gardens?"

"There is a fountain of particular beauty," Nigel answered. "Come, we will begin there and make our way through the maze of the gardens and back to the house." He led off, the French-woman on his left arm and Stacey on his right. He spoke of the different points of the gardens as he guided them. Then, as they made their way through a tunnel of well-trimmed hedge, Madame DuBois suddenly brought a palm to her forehead and stopped.

"What is it, Colette?" Nigel asked, concern obvious in his voice.

She shook her head. "It is nothing, really. Simply the effect of the plants on my being. I fear I have acquired a headache from the many lovely smells of these gardens. I must return to the house."

Turning to Stacey, Nigel said, "Ahead only a few feet is a garden seat. Rest there until I see Colette safely to her room. I shall return as soon as she is comfortable, and we will then continue our tour."

The Frenchwoman's expression of bitterness was plain to Stacey. The girl knew in that moment that the headache was but a ploy to remove Nigel from her presence. Smiling at the man, she said, "I shall be waiting, brother Nigel. Pray make haste. Madame DuBois does seem to be in monstrous pain."

With the words out, she turned away from the two and made her way down the path to the garden seat, a satisfied feeling taking her. Touché, Madame, she said to herself. Though inept at such things, I do believe I am learning your methods. She was chuckling as she came to the seat and prepared to wait.

It was a full thirty minutes before Nigel returned to say, "Very well, little sister, let us away through the gardens of Essler House." Placing her arm in his, he led her off through the gardens.

Stacey found herself curious about what had taken place while he had been away from her. Speaking in what she hoped was a normal tone, she asked, "And is Madame DuBois feeling better?"

He shrugged, saying, "The headache was still with her when I saw her to her room. It amazes me that she should be so affected. She had no such condition when we were surrounded by flowers in France."

"Is she to remain in London long, Nigel?"

Again he shrugged. "I have not spoken of it with her. I was surprised that she came here at this time. It is unusual."

"How so?" Stacey asked, genuinely curious. "Her desire to see the shops of London seems natural enough to me. I find them interesting beyond description."

He nodded. "True, but Colette has seen them many times and this, of all seasons, is the finest in

France. I wonder she would leave that beauty for this or any other place at this time."

Stacey held her tongue, thinking that as the duchess had said, Nigel was truly blind in respect to women. The talk shifted to the gardens, and she soon found herself happily engrossed in every word he said to her. Disappointment struck her an hour later when the house came into view again and she realized the tour was over. Facing him, she smiled up into his eye, saying, "Well, brother mine, there is no one I would choose for a guide other than you. It was lovely." Then without warning, she raised to tiptoe and placed a kiss on his cheek.

For a long moment following the caress, he stood looking down at her without speaking. Then, a smile breaking over his face, he said, "Ah, the wages of the garden guide have gone up, I see."

Color rose to her face, and she dropped her eyes. "There is nothing wrong with a sisterly kiss to show gratitude for a service performed," she got out. "I must hurry to the house. The duchess spoke of a hairdresser arriving this afternoon." She turned from him and fled, her embarrassment at what she'd done a heavy weight on her thoughts.

Behind her Nigel stood without moving for several minutes, his eye on her running figure, a thoughtful expression on his face. Finally, with a shake of his head as if to clear it, he followed her and entered the house.

"Well, Nigel," the duchess said when he entered. "And was the tour of the garden pleasant to all?"

"What?" he asked, her voice pulling him from his deep thoughts. "Oh, yes, Mother. Stacey has eyes that are ever hungry for the beautiful and new. She is amusing to watch."

"And Madame DuBois?"

"Colette? She came down with a damning headache before we had barely started through the gardens. The odors seemingly affected her. I returned her to her room and then proceeded to show Stacey the grounds."

The duchess nodded, a smile playing at the corners of her mouth. "Well, the child arrived only in time for the hairdresser to begin his work. If Madame DuBois is ill, I will not ask her to comment on the style of Anastasia's hair. You had best see to your own preparations, Nigel. The guests will be arriving in a short time. The dinner is prepared for forty, and you must be at the head of the table. Go now and prepare yourself."

"Yes, Mother," he said with a bow. "When you speak so, I feel as much a child as Stacey. Will there come a time when you will trust me to know what is to be done about such things?"

She laughed at the question. "Certainly, my son. That time will be when you find it in yourself to realize that parties such as this and associating with those you do not particularly care for are a necessary portion of your position. Now, go."

Chuckling, he left her and made his way up the staircase. Behind him the duchess smiled to herself and muttered aloud, "He had forgotten the

DuBois woman was a portion of the walk. Good. He is not entranced past the point of recovery."

Stepping into the great hall, she sent a glance around the room, checking the preparations. Then she made her way to the kitchens to ascertain what the cooks had done and assess the progress of the meal. Satisfied with the preparations, she returned to the front of Essler House and was in time to meet the dressmaker as the butler greeted her.

"Ah, your grace," the tradeswoman said, "I have come myself with the gown. The fitting will, perhaps, show the necessity of a tuck here and there to bring it to perfection."

"And were the alterations of such nature as to be reasonable?" the duchess asked.

A smile broke over the face of the seamstress. "They were as you suggested, your grace. You will see."

The duchess nodded. "Very well. The girl is with the hairdresser at this moment. Come, I shall take you to her and then I must prepare myself for the party." So saying, she led the woman up the stairs to Stacey's room and knocked at the door.

Cora opened the door and smiled at them. "The girl has lost the length of her tresses, your grace. Even now, he fashions the remaining hair in a way to best set off her facial features. The man is a wizard."

"Excellent," the duchess remarked, stepping aside to allow the dressmaker to enter the room. "When the efforts with the hair are complete and

Stacey has seen to her toilette, she will model the gown to ascertain if there are any further alterations to be done. I will return when I have seen to my own preparations."

"Yes, your grace," Cora answered as the duchess turned to leave. "My thanks for all you do for her, m'lady."

"The pleasure is mine," the duchess said over a shoulder as she left.

Closing the door, Cora sent a glance at Stacey, who sat quietly in front of the mirror under the ministrations of the hairdresser. Then she led the dressmaker to the bed and had her lay the wrapped gown thereon.

"She will be lovely in the gown," the woman said, stretching the wrapped garment out carefully.

A dubious expression on her face, Cora said, "The girl was not impressed with the gown, it seemed. Let us hope the choice was a correct one."

"Ah, have no fear," was the retort. "The gown will be nearly as lovely as she is herself."

"Cora," Stacey called. "It is done. Come tell me your thoughts."

Crossing to stand before the girl, the abigail studied the transformation. The auburn hair, which had reached a point some inches below the girl's shoulders, was now barely shoulder length. It sparkled with highlights brought on by some magic of the hairdresser and the edges were turned under into a soft roll. Where before there had been only an accidental stray strand of hair on the girl's forehead, there now rested soft bangs cut exactly to the symmetry of the eyebrows beneath them. The fresh, innocent face was likewise framed in the soft highlights of auburn loveliness.

"Ah, you are lovely, Stacey," Cora breathed.

"A simple matter to accomplish when one has such beauty to begin with," the hairdresser said. "Would that all my subjects were of such loveliness. My job would be ever more rewarding."

Stacey blushed under the compliments. "Thank you, kind sir. The magic concealed in your scissors would, I feel, transform an ogre into a beauty."

With a bow the hairdresser gathered his equipment and left the room. As the door closed, Stacey clapped her hands together and peered at herself in the mirror. "Ah, Cora, such a change. I do begin to appear as an adult, I believe."

"And a very attractive one," the abigail agreed. "Now, come. You must see to your toilette. The hour of the party draws near, and the gown must be tried to assure the alterations are correct."

Nodding, the girl stood, her pleasure with the hairdo leaving her at the thought of the gown and its severe lines. "Very well, Cora. I shall hurry."

Twenty minutes later, wearing only the lightest of undergarments, Stacey turned to the dressmaker, saying, "May the lovely hair arrangement make up for anything the gown lacks. Let us confine me in the thing."

A smile rode the face of the dressmaker as she pulled the wrappings from the gown. At that moment there was a knock on the door and Cora crossed to open it. The duchess stepped into the room, saying, "Good. I am in time for the showing. Come, child, make haste. I would view the results of my efforts."

Stacey nodded and turned back to the dressmaker who stood holding the yellow gown across her arms. The girl's eyes opened slightly when they fell on the material. Then as she studied the dress, she suddenly turned to face the duchess. "The gown bears little resemblance to the one chosen for me by yourself and Madame DuBois, m'lady."

"Nonsense," the duchess smiled at her. "It is the very same gown. Only the alterations make it appear different in your eyes. Put it on, child. Cora and I would see you in it."

Happily the girl swung around and allowed the dressmaker to assist her in donning the gown. When the fabric was about her and buttoned up the back, she sighed and turned to the mirror. "Oh, m'lady," she got out as her hands went to the low-cut bodice where earlier the constricting ruff had been.

"And what do you say, Cora?" the duchess asked. "Is it not a proper gown for one such as our Anastasia?"

Cora stood staring at the gown and the girl in it. "I had understood it to be of ruffed neck and of long sleeves, your grace. This cannot be the gown which was described to me."

"It is," the duchess assured her, "with but a few

177

minor alterations." Her glance went to the dressmaker. "Well, is anything else required?"

The tradeswoman shook her head. "Nothing. The girl is beautiful."

Stacey was oblivious to all that was going on around her. She was caught up with the image staring back from the mirror. Again her fingertips went to the low-cut bodice and the telling swell of her upper breasts. She sighed softly in disbelief.

"Well, girl, what is your opinion?" the duchess asked. "Will the gown suffice?"

Turning, Stacey smiled and spread her hands in wonder. "Ah, m'lady, that you would do such a thing is marvelous. I shall never in all my life be able to properly thank you. I had thought . . ."

"Of course you had. However, it was as I said: we could depend on Madame DuBois directing us to the best possible gown for you. I am certain she meant for the ruff to be removed and the sleeves to be shortened. She simply neglected to make mention of it."

Stacey's smile was broad. "Of course, m'lady." She pirouetted happily, saying, "This is to be the most beautiful evening of my life."

Laughing at the girl, the duchess turned to leave, saying, "See that you do not find your way down the stairs until I send word, child. I would have the proper ones present before you make your entrance."

"Oh, yes, m'lady," Stacey got out before the duchess left the room. Then she turned to find Cora and the dressmaker watching her. "Oh, is she not the most wonderful friend anyone has ever had!" she exclaimed.

Laughing, Cora agreed. "And I believe you should show proper gratitude to the lady who has brought about the change in the gown you so feared, lass."

Stacey crossed to take the dressmaker's hands in her own. "You—as the dressmaker—are a magician. I cannot begin to thank you for what you have done."

The seamstress chuckled. "Though I have been in the business for a number of years, I was taken aback when the duchess returned to my shop to instruct me in the removal of the ruff and the sleeves. She is the one who deserves your thanks. Wear the dress in good health. Now, I must be going. I have absented myself from my business too long."

"Again, thank you," Stacey said as the woman left the room.

"Ah, child," Cora said dreamily, "you are suddenly all grown up from a lovely child to a beautiful lady. There will be none present at the party who will be able to keep their eyes from you."

A dreamy look entered the girl's eyes. "May Nigel find pleasure in the sight of me, Cora. That is my only prayer."

Nodding understanding, the abigail said, "Yes, well I think he will find himself taken with you. Now the guests are arriving. Come, just a touch of color to your lips and you will be prepared to take yourself below. Hurry, lass. The call from the duchess will come at any moment."

For the next five minutes Stacey paced from mirror to doorway anxiously. Finally, when she thought she must surely burst, a tap came at the door.

Moving swiftly to open the door a crack, Cora asked, "Who knocks?"

"Her grace requests that Lady Anastasia attend the gathering in the great hall," a servant answered.

"Very well," Cora said, turning to send a smiling glance at the impatient and frightened girl. "Come, child. Your moment is here. Hold your head high. There will be none below to match your beauty."

"Oh, Cora," the girl said in anguish. "I am afraid I surely must blunder in some way."

"Nonsense. Shortly I shall be within seeing distance, should you find yourself in need of me. Now, go. This truly is your night."

With a silent prayer for guidance through the next few hours, the girl left the room and made her way down the stairs. The murmuring din of voices came to her before she had traversed half the distance of the stairway. Then she gained the ground floor. Swallowing back her desire to turn and run, she made her way toward the sounds of discussion.

The confusion of guests massed into the great hall shook her. Everywhere her glance went, groups of men and women stood talking. Then, as she stepped her first pace into the hall, a young man to the right of the doorway exclaimed, "Oh, I say, that is truly a bit of excellence."

Heads turned in response to the statement. Voices silenced and suddenly, as if instant death had overcome all, the hall was quiet. Every eye rested on Anastasia Griffith.

I shall this instant die, she told herself, wishing for a place to hide. Then a hand touched her arm.

"Be at your ease, little sister," Nigel told her softly. "There are none here who will harm you. Look at them. You have captivated them, each and every one."

Her eyes had been on his face since his first word. The expression he wore more than fulfilled the prayer she had made earlier in the bedroom. "And will I be acceptable, Nigel?" she asked in a rush of words.

He threw back his head and laughed. When he'd controlled himself, he made a sweeping gesture with a hand toward the crowd of watchers. "You are beyond lovely, Stacey. Do you think those eyes staring at you can believe anything else? There are many who are envious, which is as it should be. But there are none among them who wishes you any but well. Come, gather your wits together." Turning, he faced the throng. "Friends," he announced in a loud voice, "I have the extreme pleasure of introducing one who is as a dear sister to me—Anastasia Griffith."

Color flooded into her face and she fought to catch her breath. Then Nigel had her arm and was leading her through the crowd to bring her face to face with the duchess.

A satisfied expression rested on the features of the old woman as she sent a glance around her guests and then brought it to bear on Stacey. "A coup if ever there was one," she said for their ears only.

"My brat of a sister has, in secrecy, become a flower in full bloom," Nigel said. "You are to be complimented, Mother. You will have not only the young swains at her feet but the rest of London as well." He turned, searching with his good eye. "And where is Colette? She should see what her assistance has brought about."

The duchess smiled slyly at Stacey. "I noted her in the far corner with Lord Willmuth only moments ago. But, no matter. Take Stacey around and be certain she meets those of standing who would qualify as suitors."

The order caused a moment's hesitation in Nigel. He cast a glance at Stacey and, with a slight shake of his head, said, "Ah, younger sister, there is no one present worthy of your beauty. But, come, the introductions must be made before we take our places at the table."

The following thirty minutes became a jumbled mass of names and faces for the girl. She struggled vainly to remember each and every one, but found herself aswim with the very vastness of the chore.

"Be at your ease, Stacey," Nigel whispered. "It is not required that you remember the names. They will certainly remember yours. And, they do not, at last report, bite little girls."

Before she could make answer, a servant called that dinner was served. The next instant she felt

Nigel's hand at her waist turning her. She looked up with a question in her eyes.

"You shall sit on my right during the meal," he told her, again sending his searching glance around the hall. "I wonder what has become of Colette. She must sit on my left. I would have the two beauties of this gathering within easy reach."

The duchess approached at that moment, saying, "Nigel, Madame DuBois stands near the door in discussion with several ladies. It would well suit if you were to seat her at the table since your introduction of her was so meager."

A spot of color appeared above his neckcloth. "Mother, Collette is not impressed with such things. She realizes this is to be Stacey's evening and prefers not to be noticed overmuch. But you are correct. I was searching for her to place her at my left. Come, Stacey. Let us locate her and seat ourselves that the others may do so."

They found the Frenchwoman where the duchess had indicated. When Nigel spoke her name, she turned quickly to smile at him. "Ah, chéri, I had thought you gone."

Nigel chuckled softly. "Hardly that, Colette." He drew Stacey forward. "Place your eyes on the results of your efforts, Colette. Does my little sister stun all present or does she not?"

The smile was still on the woman's face when she met Stacey's glance. The glint in her eyes, however, belied any warmth indicated by that smile. "She is, of course, as I knew she would be." She hesitated a long moment studying Stacey, then added, "The gown is not as I recall it. The alterations were more extensive than imagined."

Stacey smiled at her and dropped into a half curtsy. "My thanks to you for your choice of the gown, madame. Though I doubted the selection at first sight, I find you were indeed correct in your choice." Her eyes came up and she added, "The silver brocade you wear is lovely."

The red tinge of anger in the woman's face was only barely apparent to the girl as she straightened from the curtsy. Then, before either of them could say another word, Nigel had his arms linked in theirs saying, "Come, Colette. You shall grace my left at the dinner table."

The dinner was a form of exquisite discomfort for Anastasia. Each time she raised her glance from her plate, she was aware of the acid glance of Madame DuBois upon her. At the same time she was also aware of the admiring glances from others around the table. Her evening was complete.

During the second course of the meal, a servant stepped into the hall to bend close to the Frenchwoman's ear and murmur something to her. At her nod the servant passed her a folded slip of paper and departed. Casting a glance at Nigel, she explained, "A message from my cousin in Paris, chéri." Unfolding the slip, she spent a short moment reading it and then refolded it. Placing it under the silver bracelet she wore on her right wrist, she said, "I must return to France within a few days, Nigel."

"Bad news of the family? If there is anything I can ..."

"No, no," she said with a wave of her hand. "It is only that the DuBois fortunes may once again be available to me if my cousin's report is correct. There can be nothing done immediately. I shall take my leave of your pleasant surroundings within two days. Do not concern yourself, chéri. I shall return at the earliest possible moment and we will again be together."

The telltale spot of color appeared at the duke's neckcloth. He nodded. "We shall miss you at Essler House, Colette. Stacey could have divined much of being a woman from you. I shall see to your passage home, tomorrow."

The news that the Frenchwoman was to leave sent a thrill of elation through the girl. Her eyes conveyed that happiness when she met those of her foe. She smiled, saying, "Nigel is correct, Madame DuBois. Already I have learned much from you. I feel you are an excellent teacher."

The older woman nodded, a near-frozen smile on her lips. "And you an apt student," she returned with a trace of bitterness detectable only by the girl.

Nigel stood, lifting his wine glass. "Friends," he called down the length of the table, "I have this moment learned that my good friend and ally, Madame Colette DuBois of France, must of necessity take her leave soon. Join me in toasting both her and her country." Tipping his wine glass, he drank deeply. All along the table voices of agreement sounded as the wine was taken.

When all had drunk, Nigel again raised his glass to say, "And a second toast to the lovely Anastasia. May she take all of London as she has taken this gathering tonight." He had the cup to his lips when the servant returned to stand beside his chair. Completing the toast taking, he gave his attention to the servant, and, after a moment, turned back to his guests. "I must beg my leave of you for a short moment, friends. Pray continue with the meal. I shall return within minutes." Turning, he smiled at Stacey and left the room.

As Nigel left the room, Stacey met the troubled glance of the Frenchwoman. "Something is amiss, Madame DuBois?" she asked softly.

"What?" the Frenchwoman asked, her attention coming to bear on the girl. "What was it you asked?"

"By your expression, I thought something to be amiss, madame."

"No, nothing. I only wonder of the reason for Nigel's leaving."

Stacey nodded and would have spoken had not the duke reentered the room at that moment, a troubled expression riding his features. Nearing the head of the table, he raised a hand for silence and said, "Friends, this has truly been a night of ill reports. First the leaving of my dear friend Colette, and now, news of the worst kind has been delivered to me. Napoleon has escaped his exile at Elba and has returned to marshal his forces in France. I must take my leave of you. The War Council will meet as soon as possible. Any of that number present take note and attend me in my study." With that, he turned and would have left, had it not been for Madame DuBois reaching to clutch his arm.

"Ah, Nigel, truly the worst news imaginable. And is it possible I might be allowed to sit within the conference of the council? Too many hours and days have I fought to be left out of the planning of this."

For a moment he stood in hesitation. All along the table, men were saying their apologies and leaving their chairs to join him. Finally he shook his head. "It would be best if you were to await the completion of this, Colette. I will inform you of our decisions immediately upon our closure." He paused, then added as if to himself, "There can be no answer but to again suppress the little emperor." Then he turned and left the room, the members of the War Council following in his wake.

Silence held the remaining diners at the table. Then the duchess stood, saying, "Though I dread saying so, I fear the pleasure of the evening has fled. Those of you who wish to continue with the dance and celebration must consider Essler House as your own. I must, of necessity, prepare myself to assist my son when the decision concerning Napoleon is arrived at." So saying, she left her place and came along the table to a spot directly behind Stacey. Bending to speak into her ear, she said, "Anastasia, our Nigel is truly in anxious straits. It is my feeling that few will remain, but I ask that you act in my stead as hostess. When the matter is decided, Nigel will wish me as sounding board for whatever ideas must arise."

Swallowing hard at the responsibility thrust upon her, Stacey nodded. "You honor me, m'lady. I shall be happy to remain until the last of the guests depart. I only wish I were of such knowledge as to assist Nigel in his time of trial."

"Well said," the duchess told her. Then, with a nod at Madame DuBois and the rest of the gathering, she left the room, calling for servants as she went.

Within minutes of the duchess's leaving the dinner table, carriages were drawn to the front of Essler House and troubled guests began taking their leave. Stacey stood at the door as hostess, wishing each guest well and seeing them on their way. Concern for the duke filled her mind and body. She was genuinely relieved when she spoke the proper words to the final departing guest and turned to make her way to her bedroom.

Suddenly, from the great hall, Madame DuBois appeared, an expression of deep thought again on her face. She passed within several feet of Stacey without taking note of her and made her way to the stairs.

Though curious about the woman's actions, Stacey mounted the steps, involved in her own thoughts of how this crisis would affect the duke. Midway up the stairs, she heard the closing of a door and realized the Frenchwoman had secluded herself in her bedroom. As she attained the top step, her eyes caught the pale of white paper against the dark brown of the carpet. Bending, she picked up the scrap and undid its folds. Written thereon in a simple hand was the capital letter "B" and the word "is." She stood looking at the meager writing for a long moment before again folding it and proceeding to her room. She was at the door when Madame DuBois stepped from her bedroom, an anxious expression riding her face.

"Yes, madame?" Stacey asked.

"The note from my cousin," the Frenchwoman said, her glance scanning the carpet of the hallway. "I seem to have misplaced it. I distinctly recall placing it under my bracelet, but now, it is gone."

Holding out the folded slip of paper, Stacey asked, "Is this it, madame? I just this moment picked it up from the carpet."

Relief showed on the woman's face as she accepted the note. Then, suddenly, her expression changed to one of cautious suspicion. "My cousin borders on the illiterate, as you know—having read the note. He knows little of written language and must use symbols and initials to speak of family and problems."

An overriding caution took Stacey. Hesitating only a second, she answered, "I would not know, madame. I only this moment retrieved the paper. It is not my manner to read that which does not concern me." She turned to enter her room, aware of an alien expression on the Frenchwoman's face.

"You and the duchess have done your work well, Anastasia," Madame DuBois said as Stacey turned the lever to open her door.

"Madame?" she asked, turning to face her. "I do not understand your meaning."

A bitter smile took the Frenchwoman's face. "I believe you do, Anastasia Griffith. You have captured Nigel's heart and are aware of it." She shrugged. "Well, so be it. We can only make the attempt. May your days with him be as happy as those he and I spent together in France." A smile broke her face. "My best wishes. For no matter what you believe of me, I do realize when I am bested." Her hand came forward in a gesture of friendship.

Utterly confused by the change in the woman, Stacey accepted the hand, saying, "I love him, Madame DuBois."

The older woman nodded. "And he, you, Anastasia. I realized it the moment of our meeting. See to it that you take good care of our Nigel." With that she turned, the note in hand, and left Stacey standing in wonder.

Finally, after several moments of confused thoughts, the girl turned to enter her room, telling herself that she had, in her farm-girl ignorance, completely misjudged the woman. It was not in me to believe she would ever accept such a thing in such a manner, she told herself.

She would have mentioned the incident to Cora, but after a moment's thought, realized the abigail was most certainly below assisting the servants in removing the remains of the dinner. It occurred to her at that moment that someone should be present to advise those servants in their labors. She turned to leave the room to return to the great hall. Upon opening the door, she became aware of Madame DuBois stepping silently from her room to move quickly toward the rear stairs.

Without a sound Stacey closed the door and stood for a moment in wonder at the surreptitious manner in which the woman had made her way along the hall. As if she did not wish to be seen, she thought, moving to a window to look down upon the Essler grounds. She was there for only a moment when a paleness she immediately identified as the silver brocade of the Frenchwoman's gown came into view at the garden edge. Ah, she told herself, she wishes to walk alone with her problems. The gardens are the ideal selection for such things. She was about to turn away from the window when a darker shadow stepped from the shrubs below to join the silver-gowned figure. It took only a moment to determine that the newcomer to the gardens was a man. She turned and hurriedly made her way from the room and down the stairs to search out the duchess.

It was some ten minutes before she came upon the woman in the library. At her entrance the duchess raised her glance from a shelf of papers before her on the desk. "Yes, Anastasia. What is it?" she asked.

"I am concerned, m'lady, about Madame DuBois."

The duchess frowned. "There is much to be concerned with this night, child. Therefore the ups and downs of your romantic attachments with Nigel must wait until a more opportune moment presents itself. Nigel will have no time for such thoughts now that his predictions concerning Napoleon have come true. Contain yourself. He will again notice you when this is over."

Stacey shook her head and moved forward. "It was not in me to consume your time and thoughts with such things at this moment, m'lady. When I made mention of the French one, I referred to her strange actions within the past hour."

The duchess's expression changed to one of curiosity. "Strange actions? What actions do you speak of, Anastasia?"

"It is likely nothing more than my own imaginings," she answered, "but as I made my way to my room following the departure of the last guest, I did come upon the note delivered to the madame. It lay on the carpet where she had dropped it." She lowered her eyes in embarrassment and added, "I confess I opened it and read it. It was most confusing."

The duchess nodded and remained silent, waiting for her to continue.

"I . . . I understood it to be a note from a cousin calling for her return to Paris on family matters. But there was nothing of family matters or Paris upon the paper."

The interest in the face of the older woman sharpened. "Nothing of either?" she asked.

"No, m'lady. Only the capital letter 'B' and the word 'is.'"

"That is all?" was the instant question. Then, "You are certain of this?"

"Yes, m'lady," Stacey answered, puzzled by the new attitude assumed by the duchess.

"You have the note?"

Shaking her head, Stacey said, "No, m'lady. As I refolded it and made to enter my own room, Madame DuBois came from her room, asking about the message. I gave it to her, and she indicated her belief that I had read the contents. I denied it with a lie. It is not my natural bent to intrude in another's privacy, and I know of no good reason why I did so."

The duchess sat in deep thought for a long moment before asking, "And the woman is now in her room?"

"Oh no, m'lady. Only moments after entering my room, it occurred to me that I should be present in the great hall in your stead to advise the servants. I made to leave my room and noticed the Frenchwoman going quietly toward the rear stairs. Since I could fathom no reason for such a thing, I did not make my presence known but crossed to my window to think. While looking down upon the gardens, Madame DuBois came into view and was shortly met by a darker figure I took to be a man." She hesitated, then added, "There is another strange thing I did not mention, m'lady."

"And that is what," the duchess asked, getting to her feet.

"When I'd returned the note to her, she offered me her best wishes for happiness with Nigel and admitted defeat in her plans to make him her own."

Stopping in mid-stride, the duchess stared at her. Suddenly the old eyes narrowed into slits, and she nodded as if coming to a decision. "You have done well to come to me with this information, child. Now, return to your room and remain there. I must hasten to speak with Nigel." So saying, she swept past the girl and out of the library.

Confused beyond belief, Stacey followed the woman from the library and made her way up the stairs to her room. She was in deep concentration when she pushed open the door and suddenly became aware that she had stepped into near-total darkness. For a moment she hesitated, and in that moment a strong, rough hand settled over her mouth and an arm of steel encircled her body to lift her from the floor.

CHAPTER FOURTEEN

Alarmed by the possibilities of what the girl had read and seen, the duchess made her way quickly to the door of the study and rapped. Moments later Nigel opened the portal to say, "Mother, unless it is of extreme importance, I must beg off anything for the moment. We in this room may well decide the future of all Europe."

Nodding, the duchess pushed her way past him. "I am aware of the importance of your meeting, Nigel. It is for that reason I must disclose information only recently given me by our Anastasia."

"Ah, little sister. Her evening is ruined. But there is no time for such innocent problems at this moment."

Sending a harsh glance at him, the duchess turned to face the men gathered in the study. "Though my son infers that she is incapable of serious thought, the little sister to whom he refers has, only moments ago, given me information which I believe you will deem important to your discussion." She hesitated, waiting for any of them to speak. When no one made move to do so, she relayed the information given to her by Stacey.

"What can it mean?" Nigel asked of no one in particular.

Grimacing in disgust, the duchess snapped, "It means, son Nigel, that you are blind as all men are in matters of women such as your Colette. She is a spy for Napoleon. The 'B' can only refer to Bonaparte and the word 'is' to the fact that he is again on French soil and about to perform his own brand of devilment once again." She paused to raise a finger in his direction. "Recall, if you are not overly confused by the rustle of skirts, that she did receive the note before you were given notice that Bonaparte had returned." She again sent her attention to the others in the conference. "Well," she demanded.

To a man they looked to the duke. He, with shaking head, said, "I cannot believe such a thing of Colette. She was a trusted ally during the recent war. She could not have reason to do such a thing. And why come here if she were as you suggest, Mother?"

"Men!" the duchess exclaimed. "It is a miracle the world progresses at all with such persons at the helm. Use your head, son. What other reason could she have had but to be present when the news of Napoleon arrived. You are advisor to the War Council. To know of your decision the instant that decision was formed is worth an empire to Bonaparte."

Grudgingly the duke nodded agreement. "There seems to be no other explanation, Mother. You are correct, I fear. It does cut me deeply to make such an admission. She was dear to me at one time." He straightened suddenly, his glance going to the other men, then back to the duchess. "You say she is even now in the gardens in clandestine meeting with another?"

"She was," the duchess retorted. "Though unless there was much to discuss, you have wasted time enough for her to have traveled half the distance to France." She turned and marched past him from the study, her regal head held high, her back rigid.

Behind her Nigel snapped, "Gentlemen, several of you make your way out the front and around the garden perimeter. The rest of you come with me. If it is as my mother suggests, we are duty bound to capture the two of them. Come." He stepped from the study and nearly ran headlong into Cora.

"Oh, your grace," the abigail gasped. "Have you noticed Stacey about? She is not in her room and the light is extinguished. She seems to be nowhere within the confines of Essler House."

For a moment he stood staring at her. Then, as if a devil had taken him, he ran headlong for the gardens, calling over his shoulder as he went for the others to move to their positions with all haste. At the sounds the duchess stepped into view from her drawing room. "Mother," Nigel demanded, "is Stacey with you?"

"Of course not," she answered. "I told her to remain in her room until this matter was completed to your satisfaction. What is about?"

Tears forming in her eyes, Cora came forward to say, "Oh, your grace, the child is not in her room. The room itself is in darkness. She is nowhere to be found in the house. I fear for her."

Stepping swiftly past her son, the duchess took the abigail by the hand, saying, "Come, let us examine the upper floor. Hurry." And to Nigel, she called, "Make utmost haste to the gardens, Nigel. Though there can be no logical reason for it, the girl may have been abducted."

When the arm had gone about her waist, Stacey had begun a futile fight against her attacker. Kicking wildly, she attempted to bite the hand which clamped her lips shut, preventing a scream. Then, without warning, a form whose silver gown reflected the hallway light stepped to position in front of her. A blow, unseen in the darkness, struck her at the temple, and she sank into the darkness of oblivion.

A pulsing throb of pain coupled with the jouncing of a fast-moving coach brought her to her senses. Seconds after consciousness returned, she realized her head was covered with a bag of coarse material. She winced in pain as she tried to move her hands and realized they, as well as her feet, were bound with strong cord. A moan of anguish escaped her lips, and she fought for a full breath within the confines of the hood.

"Our guest awakens," the Frenchwoman's voice filled the coach. "How much more time?"

"But a few minutes, madame," a rough male voice spoke. "The ship is waiting. Within the hour we shall take the tide away from England."

"Good," came the answer. "Pursuit will be no problem once they discover the instructions left by me. It should be a pleasant trip to the shores of France."

Her mind filled with racing thoughts, Stacey attempted to make sense of what she had heard. Finally, in despair, she sent a muffled plea for more air through the hood.

A laugh of extreme cruelty filled the coach. "Your comfort is of little concern to me, Griffith woman," Madame DuBois snarled when her laughing had ceased. "Had it not been for your interference, information of all Europe's battle plans would have been mine. Well, they shall be mine as yet—if your beloved Nigel wishes to see you alive again." She broke into hysterical laughter again, filling the evening with raucous sound.

Within the confines of her bonds and hood, Stacey shuddered. I am kidnapped, she told herself, and my ransom is to be the freedom of all Europe. Tears filled her eyes as she thought of Nigel and muttered a silent prayer for salvation.

CHAPTER FIFTEEN

Quickly searching Stacey's room, the duchess and a concerned Cora stepped to the hall and moved along it. Without knocking, the duchess threw open the door of Madame DuBois's room and entered. Sending a quick glance around the cubicle, she crossed to the mirrored dresser and lifted a slip of paper from its rest against a silver-mounted jewel box. She was silent for a moment as she read the message. Then, spinning around with an agility surprising in one her age, she faced Cora. "The Frenchwoman has the child. Come, we must alert Nigel." Sweeping past the abigail, she left the room and made her way hurriedly down the stairs and to the rear of the Essler House.

Her call brought Nigel running from the gardens, asking, "Is she found, Mother?"

"Not found, Nigel," the duchess told him, extending the note to him. "Abducted. The message is to you from the French one."

Hurriedly he scanned the message, his expression showing defeat as he read. Then, his jaw tightening, he turned to call to the others who searched the gardens. Moments later they were gathered around him in the hallway. Without comment he passed the note to them and stood silent while they read. When all had finished, he sent a glance around the assemblage and said, "It seems I am, indeed, a fool, as my mother suggested. I have, in my ignorance, placed all of Europe in peril. I resign myself from position on the War Council." He nodded to all of them and would have gone had they not restrained him.

"It will not do, your grace," one of the group said. "You are too harsh on yourself. We now, more than ever, need your council."

He shook his head in answer. "It would be to no avail, gentlemen. I am torn between my duty to my country and my duty to one I consider a dear friend. No decision of mine could be worthy of trust. Besides I fear my thoughts must be consumed with the rescue of Stacey. I must bring her uninjured from the hands of those who have her." He paused, his glance going to the duchess. "That I, in my ignorance, have caused such a thing to happen to her will weigh heavily on me forevermore."

"As it should," the duchess snapped. "Now, Nigel, take your thoughts from your own miseries and place them on the dual situations at hand.

What is to be done concerning the girl and Napoleon?"

Standing thoughtfully silent for a long moment, he said, "There can be no question of our aim for Napoleon." Turning to the others on the War Council, he said, "Though it pains me to so advise you, the plans we had laid previous to this occurrence must be seen to. The safety of all Europe cannot be sacrified for a single person, no matter how dear." He bowed slightly and added, "Now, gentlemen, I shall take my leave of you. From this moment all my faculties must be aimed at the safe return of Stacey." He turned from them and left the room, the duchess hard on his heels.

An anxious Cora stood waiting for them when they exited the study. With only a quick glance in her direction, Nigel ordered, "Come along, Cora. We three must see to the rescue of your mistress."

Entering the library, he turned to his mother, saying, "There can be no question of Colette's intentions for Stacey. As long as the child is in her hand, she feels safe in the notion that none of Essler will see her come to harm. Therefore I must, in all haste, overtake her before she can learn that her threat has had no bearing on the battle plans of the war conference."

"But to find such a package in the dark of night is near impossible," the duchess protested. "You cannot know where she has concealed Anastasia."

The duke bowed shortly. "Allow me to say that while you were correct concerning my earlier actions, Mother, I am now in command of my faculties. There is nothing to indicate Colette has remained in England. Rather, I believe, she is even now making her way toward the mainland of France." He paused, a hand going to the eye patch, his features absorbed in thought. "Unless I misguess badly, she considers herself safe to a degree. That being the situation, she will . . ." Here he went silent. Suddenly he turned to a shelf and withdrew a map. Spreading the chart on the desk, he bent over it, the women at his side. His finger moved from London southward and stopped. "She will, I wager, go straight for Brighton, there to meet a ship and make her way to France. Yes, that is most certainly what she will do."

The duchess frowned down at the map. "You do not believe she will opt for one of the smaller, more secluded seaports from which to depart?"

He shook his head. "As I have said, she believes herself relatively safe for the moment. The road to Brighton is faster and smoother. Colette will not sacrifice comfort unless it becomes necessary. Yes, she will leave from Brighton."

"That being so," his mother said, "you and several others can mount fast horses and possibly overtake them before they can arrange for passage across the Channel."

Again he shook his head. "You underestimate Colette, Mother. I wager a ship has been in readiness for her since she first set foot on English soil. In spite of all she has done or intended, I must give her her due. She is a skillful tactician. She has the fates on her side, also, I fear."

"How so?"

"Simply that she is aware that neither I nor any Englishman can safely sail into an open French port at this time. Unlike Colette, I must acquire entrance to the country in secrecy. I must, therefore, take myself to Hastings and contact a comrade of the war."

"But the road to Hastings is in ill repair," the duchess protested. "A carriage will be twice the time in arriving at the coast."

He nodded. "True, Mother, but I have no intention of traveling by carriage. I shall, as you only moments ago suggested, take to saddle. Once I arrive at Hastings and locate DeSans, I will gain the French coast in good speed."

"DeSans?"

"A smuggler of some talent, Mother," he informed her, folding the map. "He will see to my passage. Once on French soil I shall make my way to Rouen. There, hopefully, to find Stacey and return her to her rightful place in Essler House."

"Why Rouen, Nigel? Is it of special import?"

"To Colette, it is. It is within easy carriage distance from Paris and it was the site of her home before the war. Yes, I believe it is to Rouen she will aim." So saying, he replaced the map on the shelf and opened a drawer of the desk to withdraw a brace of pistols. Then, with a nod at the two women, he turned to leave the library. Over his shoulder he said, "Rest assured, ladies, if it is at all possible, I shall return our Stacey to Essler House."

The duchess quickly followed him, asking,

"And who will you choose to accompany you, Nigel?"

"No one, Mother," he answered, without slacking his pace. "To enter Rouen, which is friendly to both Colette and, I am now certain, Napoleon, will be chore enough for one. There will be no place for others." He left the house and broke into a run toward the stables. Behind him the duchess and the abigail stood in the open doorway, watching him until he disappeared into the darkness. Moments later they heard the rattle of horse's hooves on the drive, followed by the silence of the night.

"Fear not, Cora," the duchess consoled the concerned abigail. "Nigel will return Anastasia to us. Come, let us have tea and await word of what is about. I fear neither of us could bring ourselves to sleep at this moment."

"I doubt that I shall sleep until Stacey is returned, your grace," Cora answered, following the woman from the library. "May God add speed and safety to the duke's lot this day."

"And may his reasoning be as correct as he believes," the duchess added.

Nigel sent the horse toward Hastings at breakneck speed. Paralleling the road, he was aware only of the solid thud of the hooves as they took him ever closer to his rendezvous with the Frenchwoman and Stacey. He cursed aloud once when the horse missed its footing in the darkness and nearly tumbled. Then he entered the town of Tunbridge Wells and drew to a sliding stop at the door of a lighted inn. Hastily throwing himself from the saddle, he pushed his way through the door and sent a glance around the men assembled there.

"Welcome, governor," the innkeeper called from behind the bar. "What would you be having for your pleasure this fine night?"

Advancing to the bar, Nigel faced the gathering, saying, "Tunbridge Wells is noted for its fine horses. I would have the fastest steed available this night."

Silence followed the statement. Then, from a table near the rear wall of the place, a red-haired man asked, "And who might it be wishing my Florence Horse?"

Facing him, the duke nodded shortly. "Nigel, sir, the Duke of Essler. And sorely pressed for time."

The title brought a murmur from the crowd. A man of many years got to his feet and crossed to where Nigel stood. He peered up at him for a moment before saying, "I was shareholder for your father at one time, your grace. He was a good man. Would you take an ale with us?"

"My thanks, sir," Nigel said. "But time is escaping me. I am in dire need of a fast horse to replace the one which I have half killed since leaving London." He again turned to the horse owners who had spoken earlier. "Put your own price on the animal, sir. I'll not quibble."

The red-haired one came forward through the maze of tables, saying, "If Albert Winslow does business, the price will be a fair one, your grace.

And you shall be the judge of that after riding her. Come, it is but a short distance to the stable where she is tended." He led the way from the inn into the darkness of the night. Once outside Nigel took the reins of the winded horse and led him along as he followed Winslow.

"It would serve me well if you would allow this valiant steed place in your stable, sir," he said. "It has this night served me well."

Eyeing the horse in the pale light of the moon, the man nodded. "The animal needs a fortnight of care, it appears, your grace. Is your mission this night of such urgency to require the killing of fine animals such as he?"

Recognizing the love of horses in the man's tone, Nigel answered, "There's none in the kingdom who cares more for fine animals than myself, sir. My job this night is truly demanding of all possible from myself and the horseflesh available."

"So be it," Winslow mumbled, turning into a side street and thence into a lantern-lit stable. "There she is, sir. Florence is at being the finest mare in all of England. There's none can best her in a fair race."

Lifting a lantern from a peg, Nigel studied the animal. Finally the inspection completed, he turned to face the owner. "Name your price, man. The horse is exactly what you say. I must now be on my way to Hastings. There is, even now, an innocent life in peril through my doing."

The redhead paused, his hand to his chin in thought. "Florence is a fine animal, your grace.

She'll bring top price from any who knows animals."

Irritation fled over the duke. "Good God, man," he exclaimed, "I have told you the price is no object. I won't quibble. Name what you wish for the beast."

"Is it possible she might be returned to me, your grace?"

"What? If you desire and if it is within my power, of course. Why do you ask?"

The hand dropped from the chin. "Then, your grace, take the fine animal. If, indeed, she is returned to me still alive, I would one day visit your private stables and speak with your men. There is much which fascinates me about the titled ones and their care of their animals."

"Done," Nigel answered immediately. "And should Florence meet her death under me, you shall name a price and it will be paid along with your visit to my stables."

"As fair a bargain as a man could ask, your grace. Come, allow me to saddle her for you."

Minutes later, with Winslow's well wishes still ringing in his ears, the duke swept out of Tunbridge Wells. Once outside the town he pushed the beast to its utmost, his thought on the chore of searching out the smuggler DeSans. "Lord allow he is as proud and uncaring as always," he muttered to the night.

The town of Hastings was in darkness when he rode the faltering beast into the one business street and made for the docks. The odors of the sea were heavy in his nostrils and the constant lapping of the tide accompanied him as he found his way carefully along the unlighted dockside.

It took him thirty minutes to locate the small ungainly-appearing craft for which he searched. By the dim light of the moon he made out the single word "Rebel" on the keel of the craft and sighed in relief at the discovery. Tying the horse to a bullard, he made his way aboard the boat and picked his way carefully around stacks of line and gear to the after cabin. He rapped heavily on the door of the compartment and was rewarded by a ~~grunted demand from~~ within for identification.

"Nigel, of Essler," he called in answer. "In need of the vile wine you drink and of your services this night."

The door was thrown open before the last words were out of his mouth. A bearded green-eyed giant of a man peered at him for a moment before braying loudly and throwing his arms around the duke. "Nigel," the giant growled happily. "The one-eyed saint of the smugglers. Where have you come from?"

The strength of the man took the breath from the duke. Pushing against the bear hug, he got out, "Release me, you hairy ape." When the pressure had lessened, he added, "I've come from London this night, old friend. I am in dire need of you and your vessel."

"First we sample the wine, Nigel," the green-eyed one laughed happily. "Then, we shall go wherever you ask and bring back whatever it is you wish." Turning, he stepped back into the cabin and applied fire to a lantern. When the yellow of the light searched out the corners of the small quarters, he turned to face the duke. "You've thinned, Nigel," he said. "You've taken not enough of the wine or the bread."

"It was your blasted arms that thinned me this instant past," Nigel retorted. "Ah, DeSans, as during the war, I am glad for your villainous ways. I wonder that you have not been imprisoned, though."

A roar of laughter left the shipowner's mouth. "I, DeSans, imprisoned?" he bellowed. "For what cause, Nigel? Who gives more to the church each week? Who pays the town leaders more? Who has the fastest craft and the keenest mind among all the merchants who put to sea?"

Nigel laughed in spite of himself. "Ever the same, DeSans. Well, the keenness of your mind will be tested this night. We are again involved with Bonaparte. He is at this moment in France, rallying his troops."

The smuggler turned from a cabinet, bearing a wine bottle and two glasses. An expression of disbelief rode his face. "He escaped Elba?" he asked, and at Nigel's nod, "Damme. You claimed they would not hold him there. And is that the reason for your interrupting my sleep this night? You wish my services to squelch the little emperor a second time?"

Accepting a glass of wine, Nigel said, "Partially, old friend. However, your aid might not be required as it was before. You recall Colette?"

The green eyes sparkled in the lantern light.

"Ah, Colette, the angel," he murmured in memory. "Well do I remember her, Nigel. Had it not been for your own feelings, it would have been DeSans who warmed her on the cold nights of the campaigns. Oh, yes, I remember her."

Nigel drank deeply, took a breath, and nodded, "It is any but angel she is this night, friend. It is she I pursue."

A leer captured the smuggler's face. "And if I recall, she moves ever so slowly when you pursue, friend. Does she play girlish games with you?"

"She has abducted one who is dear to me in an attempt to force the battle plans of Europe from me. She demands that we hold in abeyance until Bonaparte is entrenched."

Again disbelief swept over the giant's face. "Colette? Colette, the lovely, in league with Napoleon? You jest, Nigel. Tell me it is not so."

"I only wish it were possible to say it, DeSans. But it is true. Who knows for what reason. Whatever the reason, she has committed this foul deed, and I must hasten to France with your help and guidance to rescue a dear friend."

The green eyes narrowed. "A dear friend of the woman type, is it?"

Nigel nodded. "She is as younger sister to me. It is through my doing and ignorance she finds herself in danger at this moment. Will you help me, DeSans?"

DeSans tipped his cup and swallowed the wine in its entirety. When he placed the cup on the table, he said, "The question is a foolish one, Nigel. Though I was unaware of your having a younger sister. My boat and my soul are yours as ever. Ask it of me and I will do it."

"The girl is not actually my sister. She is the daughter of a family friend who died. Her father was third cousin to my own. She is by way of being a ward of mine."

A slight smile captured the lips of the green-eyed one. "Ward, is it? Well, if she is past her twelfth year, she'd best watch the Nigel I knew in France." He cocked his head to the side and studied Nigel. "Or is the Duke of Essler of an age where he no longer notices the young lasses?"

Chuckling, Nigel said, "That age will come when they place me in the grave, DeSans. But, though lovely beyond the norm, she is as I stated: as a little sister to me. She is only in her twentieth year."

"Only? Well, I see the time has taken toll of you if you think one of that age to be too young to take note of. Now, what is it you would have me do?"

Tipping the cup to his lips, Nigel drained the wine before saying, "I must reach France, preferrably at Dieppe. From there I will take myself to Rouen and search out Colette and her prisoner."

"You believe she will return to Rouen? Why?"

"It was her home before the war. She has friends there who will assist her in anything she sets about."

"Which will make it difficult for you to locate her and to rescue the damsel you seek," DeSans pointed out.

Nigel nodded. "True, but there is no help for it. I must collect all my wits and assume a disguise which will keep the townspeople of Rouen from naming me to Colette."

A snort left the mouth of the smuggler. "With the eye patch, that will be no small endeavor. I will put my mind to it. Now, if we are to arrive in good time, we must set sail. Assist me at the mast." He led the way from the cabin, his step quick and sure on the deck of the ship.

"I am in your debt, DeSans," Nigel said as he followed the man. "Whatever you desire when this is completed is yours."

"I shall put my mind to that, also," was the answer as the giant hoisted the sail in preparation for leaving the coast.

"Before sailing, care must be given to the steed which brought me here," Nigel said. "Is it possible you know of someone trustworthy?"

DeSans secured the sail and turned, saying, "A moment, Nigel. There is an old man but two ships away. I will wake him and leave instructions." He jumped from the deck to the dock and disappeared in the darkness to return only minutes later. "It is seen to," he reported.

Twenty minutes later, with the wind of the Channel filling the sail, Nigel said, "A fine night for sailing. We will not be long in achieving Dieppe."

"Miles are miles and must be covered, Nigel," DeSans offered philosophically. "You were ever the one to wish an immediate end to all you attempted."

"In this matter, speed is my only ally," Nigel answered. "May the heavens offer it to me in abundance."

CHAPTER SIXTEEN

The carriage came to a jolting, rocking stop. The salt smell of the sea filled the hood covering Stacey's head. Then she was clutched by shoulders and ankles and lifted bodily from the floor of the vehicle. Any attempt to fight her captors resulted in nothing more than bringing an oath from one of the men who carried her. Minutes later she was placed unceremoniously on a wood deck.

"There she is, Madame DuBois," the male voice said. "Bag and baggage, so to speak. Shall we leave her here on the maindeck for the voyage?"

"Remove the bag from her head. She is beyond seeing anything of importance now. Quickly! Let us remove ourselves to the shores of France."

Relief flooded over Stacey when the bag was removed. She breathed deeply of the sea air before shifting her glance to the Frenchwoman. Then, hatred alive in the young eyes, she said, "You are evil beyond belief, madame."

The statement brought a near hysterical laugh to the lips of Madame DuBois. "You simpleton," she snarled when she was again in control of herself. "Evil? What is evil when compared to the conquest of all Europe. Your Nigel is a fool, and he shall pay for his foolishness. It was only by the merest coincidence that he achieved success in the earlier campaigns. Napoleon will not allow such a thing to happen again."

Stacey stared at her in disbelief. "You fought alongside Nigel," she got out. "He knew you as an ally."

"Yes, the fool," she laughed. "The warmth of a woman's body has caused many a man to err. He was and, indeed, remains a fool." Reading dismay in Stacey's expression, she suddenly broke into laughter again. "Ah, and you are a fool, also, Anastasia Griffith. It pains you to know he has lain beside me. Is it in you to think he does not crave one such as I? Bah! He is and shall always be a fool. Even now he witholds his command that would endanger Napoleon. And all because he puts your life first above all Europe's safety."

"I hate you!" Stacey cried. "I hate you as I would any vile, craven animal. You shall know God's wrath, as well as Nigel's."

"God smiles on Bonaparte," was the retort. "And I shall be his chosen one to afford him the pleasures no one else in all of France is capable of. He appreciated me as no other." She turned to call to two seamen. "Take her below and place her in a compartment where I will not be forced to look upon her."

"You shall pay for this outrage, madame," Stacey called as two seamen carried her from the main deck to a compartment and laid her on a bunk. "I would have water to drink," she said when the men turned to leave the compartment.

Eyeing her, the older one nodded. "Aye, there are the necessities you will require. I will speak to Madame DuBois of them." Then they were gone, leaving her bound and afraid.

She was aware of voices calling for sail and then of the movement of the ship as it put to sea. With the first motion of the vessel, she fell into deep despair. "Ah, I am lost," she muttered, tears flooding her eyes. "There's none can assist me now." The exhaustion of the recent hours had its way with her then, and she fell into a troubled sleep, the silver paths of tears scarring her face.

Daybreak found Nigel on deck staring in the direction of the French coast. Turning to his friend, he asked, "How many more hours, DeSans?"

DeSans thought for a moment before saying, "With the good wind which favors us, midafternoon should see us on the shores of Dieppe. I have given thought to your problem of disguise, friend. We must enter Rouen as a father and his blind son."

Nigel stared at him for a moment before saying,

219

"You shall not put yourself in danger on my account, DeSans. I welcome the thought gratefully. But it will not do."

The seaman growled at him, "And is it DeSans who is being told what he can and cannot do? Never has there been a time when an Englishman was capable of such thing. We shall enter Rouen as I have said."

Nigel shook his head. "Even if I were to allow such a thing, it would not suffice. The instant the eye patch was noticed, I would be given away. No, we must think of something else."

"What eye patch is it you speak of? Do you, perhaps, refer to the bandage over your upper head and both eyes? You are every bit as balmy as the son I shall lead into Rouen. I shall be a caring father with my addle-headed offspring. There's none who have not seen such a thing from Napoleon's escapades. It will serve us well."

A glint of deep respect came into the duke's eye. "Ah, friend of mine. You have indeed come up with a sufficient plan. But I cannot allow you to endanger yourself so. Recall that Colette knows you as well as me."

DeSans snorted. "And was it not but hours ago you spoke to me of her feeling of safety since she holds this little sister of yours? Think you she will recall me or imagine that you would make such haste to France by way of my ship? I admit to the fact that had it not been for you, she would have had eyes only for DeSans. She will not, however, imagine that I will be in Rouen in search of her."

Nigel thought about the plan for a moment and finally nodded. "Though it pains me to force you into such a position, the plan is a good one. I have stated I am in your debt. I am, now, even more so. I will not forget."

DeSans nodded with a chuckle. "I have been setting my mind on that also," he murmured.

Turning back to search the seas for coastline, Nigel answered, "Anything you ask shall be yours; make no mistake of it."

Stacey awoke to feel qualms of nausea sweep over her at the constant motion of the ship. She swallowed heavily and then called out.

Almost instantly the door of the compartment opened to admit Madame DuBois. She sent an expression of scorn at the bound girl, saying, "I was passing when your cry came to me. What is it, my simple one? Can it be you realize what is being given up for you?"

"I sicken," Stacey got out. "I fear I must part with my stomach and all it claims."

The Frenchwoman laughed. "You have the green hue of the ill, certainly. Well, though I would rather you would die in your own broth, the captain would not care for such a thing. Restrain yourself while I fetch help." Then she was gone, only to return moments later with a seaman. "I shall remove her bonds and see to her needs. Mind you stand ready should she take chance and escape me."

"Aye, madame," the seaman answered, blocking

the doorway with his body. "She'll not be getting past me."

Moment later the bonds fell from Stacey's wrists and ankles, accompanied by the harsh needlelike sting of fresh blood entering her limbs. Hurriedly she brought herself to a sitting position on the bunk and attempted to stand. Her ankles betrayed her, and she would have fallen had not Madame DuBois clutched her.

"There is little fear of your escaping, I see," she laughed as she forced the girl to stand. "Come, I will see you to the toilette." She half led, half pushed the girl to a small cubicle at the corner of the room.

Some ten minutes later, her throat burning from the sensation of vomiting, Stacey was led back to the bunk and once again bound. When the bonds were in place, the Frenchwoman stared down at her, saying scornfully, "And such a weakling is what Nigel seeks as his own. He will know many moments of regret unless I misguess." She turned to leave, then halted to add, "I may choose to favor Nigel by seeing to it you never return." Then she was gone, the seaman following her.

The final words of the woman struck deep in Stacey. She lay in awe at their meaning for some time before exclaiming aloud, "She means to have me dead. She does not mean to free me to Nigel no matter what he might do." The realization sent a quiver of fear across her and brought the beginning of more tears to her eyes. She was sobbing freely when she became aware of a bustle of movement above her on the maindeck. Then, the words "Land ho," came to her ears, and she knew they had reached the destination planned by Madame DuBois.

CHAPTER SEVENTEEN

"And you can cease your useless pacing," DeSans told Nigel. "Unless I sadly misguess, the dark edge on the horizon will be France. Shall we approach in the light of day or await the coming of dusk only hours away?"

Studying the position of the sun and the distance to the shores of France visible across the waters, Nigel said, "It will be dusk by the time we attain the shore, good friend. Is a secret landing spot known to you on these shores?"

A deep laugh escaped the seaman's lips. "There are more of such places known to DeSans than of normal ports, Nigel. If you desire one, I know the perfect spot."

Nigel nodded shortly. "Steer for it, then, friend. I would have none see us until we enter Rouen."

"It is done," DeSans retorted, bringing the ship

along a slight bit. "Would you enter Rouen in a carriage?"

The duke considered the suggestion momentarily before shaking his head in a negative answer. "For a poor father with a blind and addlepated son, a carriage would seem overmuch. Better we should arrive on foot."

"You shall arrive on foot if you desire," was the answer. "I, for one, will ride to within a short distance of the town."

"You know of a place to acquire a carriage and horses?"

"DeSans has many friends in many places," the seaman answered. "I shall see to it."

Shortly after the ship had bumped against the dock, the door of the compartment opened, and Stacey found herself being carried upward to the maindeck to be transferred to a coach. As she gained her seat in the vehicle, she stared across at Madame DuBois.

"You are now on French soil, Anastasia Griffith," the woman said. "The realm of Napoleon Bonaparte." She reached into the folds of her gown and produced a small pistol. "There will be no need of your bonds for the rest of the journey. Emille will join us shortly. He will see to untying you."

Her eyes fixed on the pistol, Stacey asked, "And do you intend that I am to die, madame?"

The Frenchwoman fixed her with a glance of interest. "Does the thought frighten you, girl?"

Stacey nodded. "I would have to be short in the

head to admit any other, madame. But I cannot see what it will avail you."

The coarse laugh of the woman filled the interior of the vehicle with sound. "You cannot see? Surely you know the feelings of a woman scorned." She shrugged suddenly. "Enough of this. The decision as to your fate has not been made. Better you be at your ease for the time you have left. Perhaps Nigel will determine a method of ransoming you from myself and Bonaparte."

"We go to meet Napoleon?" Stacey asked in awe.

"Of course you shall meet him. He will waste no time arriving at Rouen once he learns I am present on French soil. His is a desire that will drive him to me instantly. He shall determine your fate." She smiled wickedly. "Perhaps he will see something in your innocence he will wish to avail himself of."

"You can't mean . . ." Stacey got out. "You wouldn't allow such a thing."

"Ah, but yes. Men have many women in their lives. And the thought of such a thing will assist both Nigel and myself."

"Are you truly mad, madame? By what means could Napoleon's rape of my person assist either of you?"

The chuckle was alive on the woman's lips. "Why, Nigel could hardly see the same innocent he has fallen in love with once she has become a soiled flower at the hands of Napoleon. It will serve to prevent his spending a life of misery with you. As for myself, should such an occurrence take place, and should I so decide to take your life, it will make the chore even more pleasant in my knowing that Napoleon had indeed known your body."

The carriage door opened at that moment and a suave-appearing Frenchman stepped in. His glance went to Madame DeBois and the gun, then swung to the girl. "Ah, Colette," he asked in the French tongue. "Is she such a tiger you require a pistol while she is in bonds?"

"You know the language of England, Emille," Madame DuBois snapped. "Use it. I would have this one realize what the future holds for her and for all Europe. Now remove her bonds. She will be allowed to ride free of them till we arrive at Rouen."

He fixed her with an inquisitive glance and, reverting to English, asked, "You soften with age, Colette?"

"You are an ass, Emille," she retorted. "If she chooses to escape, I shall find ample reason to shoot her. Now remove her bonds and let us to Rouen. I would have Bonaparte know of our arrival."

Bending to undo the bonds which held Stacey, he asked, "And am I to understand there will be no time for us to become reacquainted, Colette? Say it is not so. I have waited weeks to again share your moments with me."

The expression on the woman's face softened slightly. "It will require a messenger to Paris for Napoleon to know we are arrived. There can be no reason to expect word before morning. We shall have this night in Rouen."

When the bonds fell from her feet and wrists, Stacey met the eyes of the Frenchman, saying, "My thanks sir. I would comment that your taste in women leaves much to be desired."

He laughed at her and turned to Madame DuBois. "Ah, Colette, you have found an admirer. Shall I split her mouth for saying such a thing of you?"

With a triumphant glance at Stacey, she said, "She is little worth such effort, Emille. Tell the driver to hasten our trip to Rouen. I would feel your warmth and skill before another hour passes."

Bending to kiss her, he said, "Yes, chérie. My passions overwhelm me at the thought." Then he called to the driver, and the coach jerked into high-speed travel with the crack of a whip.

Nigel stood silently in the front room of a ramshackle French home watching DeSans converse with the homeowner. Only moments before, upon their arrival, the room had been occupied with five poorly dressed children and a similarly dressed woman. These persons had been shooed from the room upon the homeowner's recognition of DeSans.

"True," the man told DeSans. "I can well see you are again on French soil. But I have nothing in preparation for you. The times are not what they were. There is little a man can do to support a family such as mine." His glance flicked to

Nigel, and he asked, "What is it you could want from such as me this hour of the night?"

DeSans snorted derisively. "Though it means little to you, Napoleon has escaped his exile at Elba. He is again on French soil. My friend and I travel to Paris to attempt recapture of him. We will be in need of a vehicle of some sort. Also a bandage for my friend's head and different clothes for the both of us."

The man's glance again went to the duke. "There are no clothes in my possession fitting for your friend to don. I am a poor man. There is nothing I can do for you."

"Is it your wish to remain poor?" DeSans demanded. "Come, your playacting impresses no one. You have what we need and the price upon it. Neither of us is quibbling."

The sorrowful expression left the man's face. "Ah, DeSans, you are very discerning. Tell me, why must the head of your friend be wrapped?"

"We are purchasing your assistance and your clothes," DeSans retorted, "not paying you to pry into that which is none of your affair. The binding for the head must cover the eyes and at the same time be instantly removable. See to it." He turned to Nigel. "I fear this will cost you dear, my friend. He knows nothing but his own gains."

Nigel shrugged. "The concern is as nothing. We will pay him." He paused, then added, "Half now and half on our return."

The smile which had spread on the face of the homeowner diminished at the words. "I have not mentioned what I shall require," he said.

"Then make short work of it," DeSans ordered.

The man was thoughtful for a moment, then, eyeing the duke, he said, "It appears your friend is English, DeSans. One hundred English pounds is my price for this evil you ask of me."

"Bah," DeSans snapped before Nigel could speak. "Think you I will allow you to steal from me or those for whom I care?" Turning to Nigel, he reached to pull a pistol from the duke's waistband and pointed it at the homeowner. "I would sooner put a ball through your head and take what I need," he said threateningly.

The man paled noticeably at the threat. His hands came up as if to fend off the ball which had not been shot. "It was but my first offer, DeSans. I am aware of the past debt I owe you. Come, lower the pistol and tell me what I should receive."

DeSans lowered the pistol and turned to Nigel, a question in his eyes.

"I have barely fifty pounds on my person," the duke said. "In my haste it was not in me to give conscious thought to my needs."

DeSans turned back to the man. "Thirty pounds. No more. Fifteen now and fifteen when we return."

"And," Nigel put in, "the remaining seventy pounds delivered to you by packet upon my return to England."

The statement brought an expression of hurt to DeSans's features, but he held his tongue.

The homeowner fixed Nigel with a steady

231

glance and asked, "And is your English word trustworthy?"

The pistol again came to bear on his heart. "You request death at my hand with your brashness," DeSans growled. "There is none in England who is more dependable. If he is fool enough to promise you the extra, you shall receive it. Now apologize for your suspicions and let us get on with this."

"My sincere apologies, m'lord," the man said, then turned quickly to yell for his wife to attend them.

The carriage rolled to a stop at the steps of a large, well-tended home. Stacey, her thoughts on her desperate situation, was jerked back to reality by the hand of Emille settling on her wrist.

"Come," he said. "We are arrived."

"Where are we?" she asked, her glance studying the grounds of the home.

"You are at my home," Madame DuBois informed her. "Given me by Napoleon, before the rogues of England charged it to themselves to battle him."

"But Nigel said you were of the titled French. Your husband . . ."

"Fool!" the woman burst out. "I have no husband. But thanks to Napoleon, I am as the titled French. This hamlet was given to my charge by him." She had an expression of pride on her face as she uttered the words.

"Then, you were never an ally to Nigel," Stacey

sighed. "You did put lie to everything you said to him. And he believed you."

Stepping from the coach, Madame DuBois chuckled. "Yes, he believed—as did others. What better way to know of what is afoot than to bed with those who make the decisions? Enough! Come into the house. Emille, see that she does not attempt to make off." She turned her back on them and mounted the steps to the house.

"Come," Emille told Stacey. "And, though it be nothing to me, you would best restrain your tongue. You anger Colette. She is known to be ruthless when in such a mood." So advising, he helped her from the carriage and led her inside.

"To the rear room with her, Emille," the Frenchwoman ordered when the two entered. "See that she is bound securely to the bed. If there is anything she requires in the way of nature's necessities, see to it. I will await you in the study. A message must be sent to Napoleon." She left them to enter a room at the end of the hallway.

Minutes later Stacey found herself again bound at wrists and ankles. The posts of the bed acted as binding posts, and she was spread upon the surface of the bed.

Straightening from his efforts, Emille smiled down into her face. "I hope the knots are not of such as to cause you pain, chérie. You must see the necessity of your being secure. I shall see that you are called upon each hour for your needs. Concern yourself not. Your stay will be made as pleasant as I can command."

233

"I wish only to be free," Stacey said, sensing the man's mood.

He laughed heartily at this. "Make no mistake in me, girl. Your life means little to me. I see no common sense in causing discomfort where none is necessary. I will, however, do all necessary to see that Colette has her wishes. I doubt that she will require that you meet death. But—and again, mistake me not—if she so asks, I will slit your throat in the bat of an eye."

The compelling force of the words paled her into sudden fear. She met his steady glance, asking, "You love her so much?"

"More than the breath that fills my lungs," he answered. "She is mine for the most part. One can ask no more from one blessed by the gods."

"You are indeed a fool," Stacey said and instantly regretted the words. The man's face darkened, and he moved a step nearer her. He struck her soundly on the cheek.

The pain of the blow sent her senses reeling. Then, gathering her scattered wits about her, she fixed him with a tearful glance. "My sympathies are with you, sir. Though you care not for me, I feel for your situation."

"Bah!" he exclaimed, turning to stomp from the room.

As the door slammed behind him, Stacey uttered a silent prayer that death might reach her before Napoleon could.

"You should have worn the infernal thing," DeSans snarled as he attempted to refit the bandage to Nigel's head. "I doubt that it will ever regain its original position."

"Oh, hush your anger, DeSans," Nigel growled. "We are both in a state of nerves. It makes your fingers move where they should not and my mind wander in unlikely places. Here, allow me to see to my own blinding."

Stepping away from him, DeSans snarled, "It must be right. There can be no room for error at this point."

"And so it shall be," Nigel said, fitting the head wrap into place. "There. I am blinded. Does it fit as it did?"

The seaman studied him for a long moment before grudgingly admitting that it was correct. "And what of the pistols? They must be concealed beneath your coat."

"And one of them beneath yours," the duke answered, drawing a pistol from his waistband and handing it toward the man. "There can be no indication of what is to become of us when we enter the town. I would have you armed and at my back if necessary."

"Aye," DeSans said, the gruff expression leaving his face to be replaced with a smile. "It shall indeed be as old times, Nigel. Come, let us see if we can locate the fair Colette. I would have words with that one."

"You would have many things with her, I surmise," the duke retorted with a chuckle. "But words are not in your thoughts, I wager."

Laughing at the statement, the seaman took him by the arm and led him from the grove of trees where they had concealed the horses and carriage. When they reached the road, he said, "It is but a few minutes' walk into town. Pray act as a blind, idiot son would."

"And how can I act as any but blind?" Nigel demanded. "There is nothing of the light of day to pass through this bandage."

"As well," was the answer. "Darkness descends and there is little to be seen. Now we must only achieve the lesser part of the masquerade. You must become addlepated."

"And you perceive that is of no consequence, do you?" Nigel laughed.

"Your actions would leave me little else . . ." He went silent then, his grip tightening on the duke's arm.

"What is it?" Nigel whispered.

"Someone rides toward us in the waning light," DeSans answered. "Hold steady. I shall speak with him."

"Nonsense," Nigel said. "We must get to Rouen."

"Cease your muttering, blind and stupid son. I shall decide what is to be done from this moment," DeSans said. Then, in French, loud enough to be heard for some distance, he called, "Ho, traveler. We seek the limits of Rouen. Is it in you to know the distance?"

The horse slowed and came to a stop. "You are but around the curve from Rouen," came the answer. "Now, on with you. I have important work to see to."

"Oh, that is obvious, sir," DeSans answered.

"Our thanks for your assistance. Is it ill problems you hurry to solve? And if so, could we be of service?"

Nigel, in his blindness of the bandage, was aware of a haughty note in the man's voice when he answered, "I carry a message to the savior of France. I have not problems such as you could help with. Out of my way."

"You speak of Napoleon?" DeSans asked. "My son lost his senses and his sight serving him. May the good Lord see to it that you are saying he is again on French soil."

"To complete what was begun long ago," was the answer. "I go now as personal emissary of one dear to him."

A chuckle escaped the seaman's lips. "From Rouen? What possible reason could there be for any in Rouen to think that Napoleon would care to hear from them?"

"Bah! Out of my way, man. And move your idiot son. Madame DeBois will brook nothing in the manner of slowness from me. The world of France depends on me this night."

"DuBois? DuBois? It is a name I know," DeSans said reflectively. "Ah yes, the smith's widow who lives above the shop of her former husband. Does she still take the young apothecary to her bed at night?"

"Hah!" exclaimed the messenger. "Madame occupied the Chateau de Royale at the command of Bonaparte. You are indeed foolish, old man. Move yourself and your son lest I run you over."

"Of course, sir," DeSans said, pulling Nigel

from the path of the rider. "My apologies for holding you from your mission."

Nodding, the man put the horse in motion to move past them. As the stirrup came even with him, DeSans leaped to clutch the arm and neck of the rider and drag him from the horse. He dealt one solid blow to the man's head and then grasped the nervous horse's head.

"What is happening?" Nigel demanded. "Has he gone?"

"He has decided to forgo his mission this night," DeSans answered. "Stand where you are, Nigel. I shall use the leather of the horse to bind him. Then we shall proceed into the town."

"You worked the information we needed from him. Why have you struck him?"

"I see no reason to allow Napoleon more of a helping than necessary. Your concern for the little one makes you careless, my friend. Now, silence yourself. I have work to see to."

With a shake of his bandaged head in despair, Nigel silenced himself and waited patiently until the seaman's hand again took his arm. "We must make haste to this Chateau de Royale," he said as DeSans set him in motion along the road.

"First we must find its location," was the answer. "Then we shall see to satisfying both our needs this night."

"You take command, I sense. What of a plan?"

"And should I be expected to allow a blind and idiot son to command me?" DeSans asked happily. "As to the plan it is seen to. I shall care for you in your blind idiocy, son."

CHAPTER EIGHTEEN

Darkness had filled the room when the door opened and Emille stepped inside with a candle in hand. Behind him was a servant girl bearing a tray of food. He placed the candle on a bedside table and reached to remove the bonds from Stacey's wrists. "Though you bear me nothing but insult, I shall not see you starve," he said as her hands came free. "Sit up and eat. Then, with the maid as company and myself as guard, you shall see to whatever else you need."

Rubbing her wrists, she met his glance and nodded. "Very well, Emille. I thank you for your concern, though why you bother causes me wonder."

He laughed shortly. "I would have none in the madame's house go without the necessities. For this house shall become a portion of my own once

Napoleon has accomplished his aim. Then Colette and I shall reside here."

Stacey, about to retort as to his disillusionment, held her tongue. She began eating and discovered that she was indeed ravenous. When she had consumed all the plate held, she again looked at him, saying, "I would be allowed to accept your offer of the maid's company for the necessities."

"Done," he answered, moving to remove the bonds from her ankles. When the chore had been completed, he turned to the maid, saying, "See to her needs and allow her not to affect you." He drew a pistol from his pocket, adding, "Should she come from the toilette with you as shield, you both shall meet death."

Pale faced, the maid led Stacey from the room with Emille following.

"What is the noise which strikes my ear?" Nigel asked as DeSans led him along.

"An ale house alight and filled with merrymakers celebrating the return of the short emperor," his companion answered. "Ho. Contain your English tongue. Someone approaches." A moment later he said in French, "Your pardon, sir, my son and myself are in search of the Chateau de Royal. We would speak with the lady of that place. Might you direct us?"

For a moment the man studied him in silence. Then, weaving slightly, he answered, "Are you aware of the return of Napoleon, man?"

"Aye," DeSans answered. "And my son has lost his senses and his sight under the great one's command. We would speak to the Madame DuBois concerning compensation for our loss. We are but poor people."

"Ah," came the slightly drunken exclamation. "And there is none who will see to that better than Napoleon. He is the savior of all France."

"Aye, he is that," DeSans answered, a touch of exasperation in his tone. "Could you direct us to the site?"

"Come," said the native. "Let us drink to Napoleon." So saying, he withdrew a flask from his pocket and offered it to DeSans.

"Of course," DeSans agreed, taking the flask and drinking deeply. "Now," he said when he had returned the flask to the man, "the direction I seek."

Lifting the flask to his lips, the man pointed along the street they occupied. When he lowered the liquor, he said, "At the edge of Rouen. It is the large one. You cannot mistake it."

Thanking the man, DeSans led Nigel away from him, saying, "Be glad you are blind and an idiot, my son. The man was not worthy of viewing and the wine was as vinegar."

"Your concern for my welfare touches me deeply," Nigel answered with a chuckle. "Oh, to have sight of the single eye again and my hands at your throat, old friend."

The statement brought a heavy laugh from the seaman. "For all accounts we are arrived at the point when you will be allowed to dispose of your disguise. For, unless I misguess, the chateau for which we search is the large one I now see ahead." He reached to clutch Nigel's hand, saying, "Not yet, my friend. Let us be certain before you discard the safety of your disguise."

Aware of the wisdom in the advice, Nigel withdrew his attempts to remove the bandage. "Very well, DeSans, but have you considered what will occur if you rap on the door and Colette should answer?"

"It has been prime in my thoughts. Allow me to handle such a happening."

"I would be without this infernal bandage when you call at the chateau."

"It will not do. For, if it should be Colette who answers, her eyes will for the moment remain on the bandage and you. I will require that moment to act."

Grudgingly Nigel nodded. "Very well, DeSans, but make short work of it. I would know my Stacey is of a piece."

"Quiet," came the order as the seaman turned him. "We approach the entrance." The next moment he made mention of steps and led the duke carefully up them. Then he doubled a fist and rapped on the panel facing them. The instant the rap was completed, he withdrew the pistol from under his coat and dropped his arm along his side, concealing the gun behind his leg.

Moments later the door swung open and a Frenchman of meticulous dress asked, "Yes. What is it?"

"Aye, mon ami," DeSans said. "I and my blind and addlepated son search for Madame DuBois— the friend of Napoleon Bonaparte."

The man sent a glance in back of him before saying, "She is involved with important matters. What is it you wish of her?"

The words had hardly left his mouth when DeSans swung the pistol up and brought it down upon his head. Then he loosed his hold on Nigel to catch the Frenchman as he fell. "Now, Nigel. Do away with the bandage and see to your pistol. We have found the place." He lowered Emille to the surface of the porch and stepped inside the house.

Jerking the bandage from his head, Nigel drew the pistol and stepped over the prostrate Emille to follow the seaman. They came upon a maid almost immediately. Without ceremony DeSans laid the pistol barrel alongside her head and lowered her to the floor.

"You are free with your striking of women, DeSans," Nigel said as he stepped over the girl.

"I would have no one but you behind me, Nigel," came the answer. "There seems to be no one about. Let us to the rear of the place."

They moved along, throwing open doors, guns at the ready. Finally, when they had come within two doors of the rear portion of the house, DeSans threw upon a door and said, "Ah, and unless Colette has devised a new method of entertaining her guests, this must be the Stacey for whom you search, Nigel."

The girl's eyes opened wide as the grizzled seaman entered the room with his pistol at the ready and then stepped behind the door. Her eyes fell on Nigel and she jerked against the bonds which held her, saying, "Oh, Nigel. I thought ... I ..."

He was at the bedside in a moment, kneeling to place his lips against hers. When he stood to begin working at her bonds, there was an expression of confusion on his features. "Rest easy, my Stacey," he said in half murmur. "I shall free you within the moment."

"A very touching scene," Madame DuBois said from the doorway. "No, Nigel, please be kind enough to cease your efforts with the bonds, else, I fear, I shall have to shoot you."

Every eye in the room turned to her. Nigel, defeat plain on his face, said, "And, Colette, is it in you to believe you can be successful in your plans?"

She laughed at him, the gun in her hand aimed steadily at his chest. "Napoleon will arrive within a matter of hours. Then you shall see what a true man is, Nigel. He will have none of your English prattle."

"Ah, Colette," DeSans said in sorrow as he squeezed the trigger of his pistol, "I regret having to do this."

The sound of the gun firing filled the room with reverberating echoes for long moments. The ball drove the woman around and snatched the gun from her hand. Then, regaining her balance, she clutched a hand to her bleeding arm and faced DeSans. "DeSans, the smuggler, is it not?" she asked.

He bowed, the smoking pistol still in his hand. "The same, lovely Colette." He moved toward her.

"You are but a fool of a woman. Come, remove your hand. The ball did little more than graze you. You know I could not do for you." He took her by the shoulders and turned her.

"Napoleon will . . ." she began.

". . . will not receive your message," DeSans finished for her. "I have seen to your messenger. Now let us see to your lackey at the porch and your maid. Then we must bandage the arm. I would not have merchandise that is damaged."

The moment the two had left the room, Nigel turned back to Stacey, his eyes wide as if in surprise.

"What is it, Nigel?" she asked, struggling against her bonds.

Shaking his head as if to clear it of cobwebs, he said, "It is nothing, little sister." Then he attacked the bonds and, moments later, helped her to stand. "Come," he ordered. "We must be away from this place in all haste. A boat awaits us at Dieppe. We must hurry."

They left the room and were proceeding along the hall when DeSans stepped in front of them with Madame DuBois in tow. "Are we away then?" he asked.

Nigel fixed the Frenchwoman with a glance and said, "We must, of necessity, see to Colette."

"She is seen to," the seaman said. "She comes with us."

"She cannot," Nigel said. "Are you mad?"

DeSans smiled at him. "And is your word of no value, good friend? Was it not your statement that the price of my allegiance would be whatever I asked?"

Confusion rode the duke's features. "It was and I meant every word. I hesitate to . . ." He was silent for a long moment. Then, returning the smile, he said, "If such be your wish, so be it. There is, however, payment awaiting you at Essler House."

Madame DuBois jerked against the hold DeSans had on her. "You wish to make a prostitute of me," she exclaimed.

The seaman chuckled and looked down into her eyes. "And I would be tardy in such an aim if it were mine. No, I wish to make a smuggler's apprentice of you. You shall do well aboard my vessel as the nights grow colder." He turned his attention back to Nigel and Stacey. "Come, let us away from this place." Turning, he made his way from the house with his hand firm on Madame DuBois's arm.

Following the smuggler, Nigel placed his arm around Stacey's waist, saying, "Ah, DeSans was always the dreamer. But if anyone can tame Colette, it is he." He met her glance and asked, "Are you injured in any way?"

She shook her head. "She had planned that Napoleon would . . . would . . ."

"No matter," he said. "It is enough that you are free."

Leaning her head against him as they made their way from the town in the darkness, she was only too happy to agree. The warmth of his arm around her dispelled every fear she had ever known, and she thought a silent prayer of gratitude to whatever gods there were above.

Nigel called to her through the door of the ship's compartment and brought her from a sound sleep. Sitting up in the bunk, she called to him, saying she would dress and join him soon.

"It is the dark of night, Stacey," he answered. "We are, by my friend's order, to take the longboat to the shores of England. Don your clothing and let us be on our way."

The statement brought confusion to her, but she hurried to do as he ordered. When she was dressed, she stepped from the cabin to the maindeck of the ship and faced Nigel. "What is it you say of a longboat, Nigel?"

The duke sent a glance behind him to where DeSans and Madame DuBois stood at the wheel of the ship. "DeSans would have it that he not put into shore for some time." He laughed shortly and added, "Colette has met her match, I feel. We shall use the longboat to gain the shore and then we shall gather a noble beast that waits for us. Shortly I shall return you to my mother and Cora."

CHAPTER NINETEEN

The new day was dawning as they rode onto the grounds of Essler House. Dismounting, Nigel crossed to Stacey and assisted her, saying, "They are, I am certain, yet asleep. We shall have food brought to us and await them." He led her toward the house.

The door opened under his touch and they stepped inside. Hardly had they taken more than three steps when the duchess stepped from the parlor and halted, her mouth dropping, her eyes taking on the light of relief.

"Ah, Nigel, Stacey, my chidren. You have returned," she cried, moving forward to greet them.

The statement brought a squeak of disbelief from the parlor. Cora came running from the room, her manner excited, her arms outstretched toward Stacey. "Oh, Stacey lass. I'd given up hope. Oh, I cannot . . ."

"Cora," Stacey said, clasping the woman to her. "You need not have concerned yourself. Nigel has seen to my freedom."

Nigel pushed his mother away to look down into her eyes. "I would have a moment's word with you, Mother." His glance shifted to Cora. "And with you Cora, if I may. It nears the important, and I would have it done with now."

Both women sobered at his words and nodded in agreement. He turned to Stacey, saying, "Take you into the parlor, Stacey. We shall join you momentarily." Then he led the two older women toward the study.

Confused at the turn of events and the soberness of his manner, Stacey entered the parlor and dropped into a seat. Her mind was in a turmoil when the duchess, Cora, and Nigel entered the room only minutes later. She got to her feet instantly, her manner wary.

"Anastasia," said the duchess, her manner sober, "Nigel has only now announced his determination to lay waste to all the plans for your season. Though you will never forgive him, I feel you should give an answer to him."

Her eyes swung to Nigel, then to Cora. She found herself totally confused by the smile on his face. "What is it, Nigel?" she asked.

"Only that I have been a total ass," he said, moving to her. "Until my lips settled on yours in France, I was too stupid to realize where my feelings lay." He took her in his arms and said down into her face, "I have loved you from the first moment I laid eyes on you, Stacey. I only hope you will have such a dunce as I for a husband."

Her face alight, Stacey pulled from his embrace and faced him. Her eyes swung to the duchess, to Cora, and returned to him. Then, with a happy sound emitting from her throat, she threw herself forward and into his arms, saying, "Ah, Nigel, with or without chemise, I am yours forever and ever."

Sending a glance at a smiling Cora, the duchess said, "A pity the young ones cannot know their own minds, is it not, Cora? Come, let us see to tea. I do believe we are being ignored."

MADELEINE A. POLLAND

SABRINA

Beautiful Sabrina was only 15 when her blue eyes first met the dark, dashing gaze of Gerrard Moynihan and she fell madly in love—unaware that she was already promised to the church.

As the Great War and the struggle for independence convulsed all Ireland, Sabrina also did battle. She rose from crushing defeat to shatter the iron bonds of tradition . . . to leap the convent walls and seize love—triumphant, enduring love—in a world that could never be the same.

A Dell Book $2.50   (17633-6)

At your local bookstore or use this handy coupon for ordering:

Once you've tasted joy and passion, do you dare dream of

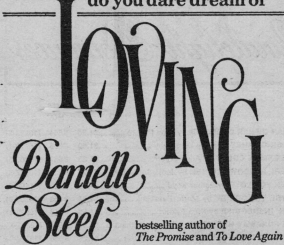

LOVING

Danielle Steel

bestselling author of
The Promise and *To Love Again*

Bettina Daniels lived in a gilded world—pampered, adored, adoring. She had youth, beauty and a glamorous life that circled the globe—everything her father's love, fame and money could buy. Suddenly, Justin Daniels was gone. Bettina stood alone before a mountain of debts and a world of strangers—men who promised her many things, who tempted her with words of love. But Bettina had to live her own life, seize her own dreams and take her own chances. But could she pay the bittersweet price?

A Dell Book ================================ **$2.75 (14684-4)**